L.I.A.R.

LOVE IS A RELIGION

KING O-HAJI

2

This book is a tribute to the relentless lovers, the fearless souls who refuse to give up on what they desire. It is for those brave enough to embrace love and risk everything for it. But above all, this book is dedicated to the one or ones who ignited its creation, stirring an uncontrollable fire within that will never be extinguished.

CONTENTS

TITLE PAGE   1

DEDICATION   2

CHAPTER 1   4

CHAPTER 2   35

CHAPTER 3   59

CHAPTER 1

Why do I keep falling for the same type of person? Every time I think I've found someone who truly cares about me, they turn out to be just another selfish and insensitive asshole. My name is Chaise Kelley, but sometimes I don't even know who that is anymore. At 33 years old, I'm starting to question if I even know who I am. A black, gay man living in Atlanta with a string of failed relationships behind me. And now, just a few hours ago, I was dumped once again. As I sit here staring out my window, all I can think about is how cliché it is for me to be another single, gay man in this city known for its vibrant LGBTQ community. But right now, all I feel is alone and lost.

In the midst of my heartbreak, I cling to the unwavering belief in love. While many have lost hope and given up on love, I hold steadfastly to its power because I have witnessed its beauty firsthand. The joy that radiates from true love is unmatched by anything else. Though at times I am tempted to abandon this faith, it goes against every fiber of my being. For I have tasted a love like no other, and it leaves me craving for more. More of him, more of that indescribable feeling that consumes me when he is near. Love may bring pain, but it also brings unimaginable bliss that makes it all worth it in the end. And for that, I will never stop believing in its magic

My phone keeps ringing, but I can't bring myself to answer it. My friends are probably calling to check on me after my messy break-up with Gage. I know they mean well, but I can't bear to hear them say "I told you so". Instead, I choose to drown my sorrows in wine and smoke hookah alone in my room. But as the wine flows, so do my emotions and I can feel myself slipping deeper into sadness. I entertain the thought of calling up a random guy to numb the pain with meaningless sex, but deep down I know it won't make me feel any better. I'm torn between wanting to distract myself and facing the pain head on.

As I sit here, my thoughts swirl in a tangled mess of confusion and disbelief. Is this some twisted nightmare that I have yet to wake up from? I pinch myself, hoping it's all just a bad dream, but the sharp pain tells me otherwise. This is my reality now - Gage has gone back to his ex without a second thought. The one who broke his heart, the one he swore he was over. And the craziest part? I didn't see it coming, or maybe I did but chose to ignore the warning signs because I was so deeply infatuated with him. But as I sit here, heartbroken and questioning everything, I can't help but wonder...where did I go wrong? Was it something I did or didn't do? Am I not enough for him?

Gage Stone. His name alone is enough to send shivers down my spine and make my heart race. At 31 years old, he's a successful photographer with an intelligence that leaves me in awe. His goofy charm and dark sense of humor draw me in, as he speaks the very thoughts, I am too afraid to voice. Standing at 5'10, he ignites a fire deep within my soul. Our chemistry is electric and when we come together, it's like fireworks exploding in the night sky. But I must not let myself get distracted by thoughts of our intense and passionate encounters, for I must stay focused on trying not to think about him, or speak his name.

You know what fuck that, let me tell you about the man who captured my heart. It all started on Facebook, as most modern romances do. His profile picture caught my attention - a stunningly beautiful man

6

with a dazzling smile, full lips, dimples that could make your heart skip a beat, and eyes that shone like pools of liquid gold. I was instantly drawn to him, unable to resist his magnetic charm. But before I could allow myself to fall too hard, I had to make sure he wasn't a catfish. Once I believed he wasn't catfish, I began sending him messages every day. However, my hopes were quickly dashed when I discovered he was already in a relationship.

So, I stayed respectful and kept our conversations friendly. But then fate intervened - after about a year or so, he and his boyfriend went their separate ways. It was finally my chance to make my move, but I knew I had to tread carefully. I didn't want to be just a rebound for him, but at the same time, I couldn't let this opportunity slip away. It was a delicate balancing act that required caution and patience on my part.

After talking on Facebook for months after his break-up, he suggested coming over to my house late one night. I knew it was risky since we had never met in person, but I thought to myself, "Why not? He could be the man of my dreams, a waste of time, or even a serial killer." Despite the risks, I decided to take the chance. As his car pulled up to my house, my nerves were all over the place. My stomach and heart felt like they were in my throat. I took one last look in the mirror and told myself, "Okay Chaise, this is it. When he rang the doorbell, I opened the door and was pleasantly surprised to see him standing there - the man from the pictures with his charming dimples and everything.

I nervously invited the man I had been dreaming about into my home, and he followed me to the kitchen. Still feeling my heart and stomach in my throat as I offered him a drink - water, wine, soda, tea...or myself. I turned red with embarrassment because I thought I had said it out loud, but fortunately, it was only in my head. He chose water, which I was relieved about since he had to drive back home. My mind was more focused on his company rather than sex. We talked for hours until he asked if I liked pecan pie. Did I like pecan pie? I loved it! And then he invited me over to his house to make one for me. Without hesitation, I said yes.

As I followed him in my car, I looked at the time and realized it was 2 a.m. we pulled into the 24-hour Walmart because he needed to buy the ingredients. For some reason, his spontaneity turned me on in ways I never even knew I could be turned on. The whole thing about him being crazy and a serial killer went out the door. Although he could have been one luring me in with a freshly baked pecan pie. He paid at the register before we both headed back to our respective vehicles. As I pulled out of the parking lot behind him, Beyoncé's' track - 'I Rather Die Young'- blared from my speakers. Of all songs this song would play as I'm headed to a complete stranger's house. We walked into his house and into his kitchen and both realized it was late and neither one of us wanted to wait up for the pecan pie. So, he promised me he would make it later in the day.

He asked if I wanted to spend the night and before I could even think, I had blurted out a hasty yes. My mind raced with thoughts of whether I could say no to this man, someone I had just met. It felt wrong, but at the same time, my body was drawn to him like a magnet. We made our way to his bedroom, and as soon as his lips touched mine, my senses were overwhelmed. The heat of his touch sent my whole body into a frenzy, and I couldn't resist kissing him back.

It was unlike anything I had ever experienced. Despite my initial intentions of portraying an innocent image, I found myself lost in the moment with him. Our passionate kiss lasted for what felt like an hour, disregarding any exhaustion we may have felt earlier. And although things could have escalated further, we both seemed content to simply be in each other's arms. In that moment, I realized that this was more than just another one-night stand - it was something special that I didn't want to end too quickly.

We had fallen asleep in each other's arms, but when I woke up, he was no longer beside me. Before I could even sit up, the door creaked open and there he was, entering the room with a tray of breakfast in hand. The aroma of freshly brewed coffee and warm pastries wafted towards me, making my stomach growl in anticipation. As I sat up in amazement, he placed the tray on my lap and asked if I wanted anything other than coffee to drink. I told him I wanted some orange juice and with a smile, he quickly went to retrieve it for me. The food looked and smelled amazing, and I couldn't believe what was happening - someone had brought me breakfast in bed. As I took my first bite, flavors exploded in my mouth, and I couldn't help but let out a satisfied moan. He returned with the orange juice and leaned in to kiss me, morning breath and all. It may not have involved any tongue, but it was still a sweet gesture that made my heart flutter. Normally, I would feel self-conscious about eating in front of someone new so soon, but with him, it felt natural and comfortable.

Being with Gage felt different. My usual worries about my appearance disappeared, knowing that this man had already seen me at my most vulnerable state - sleeping and possibly snoring. With him, I could let go of all my insecurities and just be myself. It didn't hurt that everything he cooked was delicious and I devoured every bite on my plate. He even surprised me with pecan pie, keeping his promise to make it for me. As we lounged in bed, I couldn't help but wonder where he had been all my life, and we hadn't even spent a full day together yet. We spent the whole day wrapped up in each other's arms, only taking breaks to shower, eat, and engage in intense kissing sessions. I didn't feel any pressure from him, just a sense of contentment being by his side. My phone rang non-stop, but I had put it on do not disturb mode - nothing else mattered when I was with Gage.

As each day passed, I found myself drawn closer to him. Thoughts of Gage consumed my mind, and every moment apart felt like an eternity. Even when he left for work, I would stay at his house, eagerly waiting for his return. And when he finally arrived, our kisses were like fire ignited anew. This man took care of me in every way - cooking meals after a long day's work and ensuring I was always well-fed. And it was a good thing, too, because my culinary skills were lacking. Gage had pulled me out of a dark place and brought light into my life, and I couldn't get enough of it.

As I spoke with my friends, their voices echoed with laughter and excitement through the phone. I tried to explain the happiness within me, but words failed to capture his effect on me, even to myself. Gage had rekindled my faith in love, in men. His every action brought a smile to my face, from the way his dimples deepened when he grinned, to the confident sway of his walk. All I wanted was for him to feel the same joy and warmth he had given me. And as I caught glimpses of his radiant smile directed at me, I knew that just being near him was enough; I was doing my part in making him happy. The air felt charged with an electric energy whenever we were together, and it filled me with hope and happiness for what the future held for us.

Given the recent nature of his split from his ex, I couldn't help but question if he was truly prepared to enter a relationship with me. Despite my reservations, I offered to help him retrieve the remaining pieces of his life from the home he once shared with his ex. As we pulled up to the house, I could feel my heart racing with nerves, unsure of what emotions might erupt in this volatile situation. But to my relief, there was no drama as he quickly gathered his belongings and we left. However, as I sat in the car waiting for him, I couldn't shake off the image of him inside that house with his ex, and silently prayed that he wouldn't fall back into old patterns or feelings.

I fast-forward to two weeks before Valentine's Day and found myself planning a romantic day for Gage. I ordered flowers, scheduled a spa appointment, and we spent quality time together leading up to the special day. However, two days before Valentine's Day, I didn't hear from him at all. I tried reaching out through calls, voicemails, and texts, but received no response. I convinced myself he was busy, or something was wrong, but his lack of communication worried me. I never even received a simple message saying, "I'm okay, just dealing with things."

My mind was blown, and my heart crushed. I still had the flowers sent to his address hoping I would hear something. A few days passed by, and I received this long text from Gage stating that he was so sorry and that he had gotten back with his ex. As I was reading the text everything in my body seemed to shut down except for my tears. I called my friend Stephen and all I could do was cry. Stephen was so confused because everything was going great and then Gage ghosted me.

Tears streamed down my face, and I couldn't seem to stop crying. Why did this happen? Was I too clingy? What did I do to make him leave me for his ex? I fell into a deep depression, ignoring calls from concerned friends, because all I wanted was Gage. They told me to snap out of it, but

11

it wasn't that simple. Gage had brought light into my life that I never knew I needed. Now that he was gone, I felt lost and addicted, like a drug addict without their fix. All that remained were memories, which only made the pain worse. Sometimes, I wished I could erase them entirely.

Stephen had suggested I ride by his house, but the thought made me feel like a stalker. I refused to do anything that would hurt Gage; my love for him was too strong. When you truly love someone, you don't bring unnecessary stress or drama into their life. However, I couldn't deny the urge to see this guy and drive past his house. But I needed to snap out of it before I became that crazy ex from A Thin Line Between Love and Hate. This pain was real, and it cut deep.

For the next few weeks, I woke up every day with my blackout curtains drawn tightly. Despite having a large house, I confined myself to one room, unable to face the outside world. To numb the pain and help me sleep, I resorted to purchasing pills and alcohol from the store. It was becoming clear that I had turned into an alcoholic. My phone remained in silent mode, and I only spoke with my mother, who was unaware of how low I had sunk. I didn't want her to worry about me any more than she already did. Putting on a facade and pretending everything was fine took all my energy, but I couldn't burden my mom with any additional concerns.

Who am I now? That's all I kept asking myself. I can't believe I let someone in my life again and let them turn it upside down. I was single for 3 years before I even thought about entertaining another dude. Before Gage I was with a dude for 5 years and I might as well tell you his name to get my mind off Gage but who I am kidding I'm still thinking of Gage no matter what I do. My 5-year relationship was with Aaron, and I thought he was the one but that's a whole other book. Surprisingly he and I are still very close friends because we started off as that. When he and I broke up I thought that was it. I thought my life would never be the same and honestly it wouldn't. The way Aaron loved me was everything, but I wanted more now. It wasn't perfect; I mean what is?

After our breakup I was done and afraid to love again. Although I wanted more love, I wasn't receptive and was afraid to fail again. So, I stayed single for 3 years and I would go on a date every now and then, but nothing was sticking. Who was I fooling I was looking for Aaron 2.0. Fast forward to now I want Gage or Gage 2.0. I see patterns forming and I don't like it. I opened myself up to being vulnerable. I gave my heart and Aaron had it for so long and just when I got it back FINALLY. What did I do? Give it to Gage.

Once again, my phone is ringing incessantly, and I can see that it's Stephen calling. I don't want to answer, but I know I must. The last thing I need is for him to show up at my doorstep, checking on me like some kind of babysitter. Reluctantly, I pick up the phone and hear Stephen's voice on the other end, telling me to get my lazy ass out of bed because we're going out tonight. Despite my better judgement, I get dressed and join Stephen on our night out. We ended up at a rowdy house party, where I sat in a corner and barely spoke. But Stephen keeps pushing drinks towards me and before I know it, I'm drunk and black out. The next thing I remember is waking up in my own bed with a pounding headache.

I stumbled through my house with my headache from hell and Stephen was making coffee and burnt toast in the kitchen. He shook his head at me in disappointment as we sat down to talk about what happened last night. With a heavy heart, he said, "Chaise, I am deeply disappointed by your behavior last night." My mind raced, thinking, "Did I do something terrible? Did I wreck Stephen's car or damage the host's house?" But Stephen continued, "You were so drunk that you passed out in the corner. I had to help you to my car where you proceeded to vomit, and then carry your drunken self-up to your room." I let out a sigh of relief, thinking, "Well at least I didn't cheat on someone." But Stephen's next words cut deep, "I would have preferred that you slept with someone else to get over Gage, but here you are hungover and still pining over him." We talked for a while longer before he had to leave for work. As for me, I was on medical break due to back issues. So I went back to bed, hoping to wake up from this nightmare.

I awoke to a bright, sunny day and felt an instant twinge of bitterness. I wanted the weather to match my mood - dark, gloomy, and filled with tears. Where was the rain? The pitter-patter of droplets against my window would have been a welcome sound. But instead, I had to force myself out of bed and make my way to the surgeon's office for a consultation about my back and a potential surgery date. Despite the surgeon's explanations and recommendations, I couldn't fully focus. My mind was consumed with the pain in my heart, overshadowing any physical discomfort in my back. We eventually set a date for the surgery, but I couldn't bring myself to care. It dawned on me that the sooner I had the procedure done, the sooner I could return to writing my next book - something I was dreading because it meant facing reality and trying to rebuild my life from its shattered state.

As I arrived home, the idea crossed my mind to inform Gage about my upcoming surgery. Even though he had cut off communication with me, I couldn't help but wonder how he would respond. So, after taking a couple shots of vodka for courage, I sent him a text. To my surprise, he

14

replied and expressed his desire to be there for me during this time. A rush of emotions flooded through me. Did this mean he still had feelings for me? But then again, he was still in a relationship with his ex. My mind was spinning with confusion and regret over sending that text, but at least it got a response from him.

I woke up with a smile on my face because I finally heard back from Gage, even though it was just a response to my text. As soon as I started getting ready for the day, my phone began ringing and I saw that it was my ex-boyfriend, Aaron. He wanted to check in and see how my appointment went. I couldn't help but wish it was Gage calling instead. I shared all the details of my appointment with Aaron, and he offered to help me out. Part of me wanted to say no in case Gage ended up flaking on me, but then again, I didn't want to take any chances.

Aaron and I have been close friends since we broke up and we've never discussed our dating lives. It's just easier that way. But if I'm being completely honest, I still have feelings for Aaron. However, there's something about Gage that has me hooked like never before. I accepted Aaron's offer to help, but now I'm stuck because I don't want him to meet Gage and complicate things. At the same time, I can't help but wonder if Aaron is just being a good friend or trying to get back together with me. My thoughts are all over the place, but one thing's for sure – I don't want to take any risks.

As my surgery date approached, I arranged for Aaron to drop me off at the hospital and for Gage to pick me up afterwards. Most people would be worried about having back surgery, but my mind was preoccupied with thoughts of Gage and hoping that everything would go smoothly with the drop off and pick up. On the day of the surgery, Aaron picked me up and stayed until it was over. When I woke up after a successful surgery, he was there with a smile on his face. I can't deny that his presence made me feel better, though in the back of my mind I couldn't help but think about Gage. But then again, I remind myself that I don't owe anyone anything because ultimately, I am single.

Despite Aaron's insistence on taking me home, I told him that Stephen was already picking me up and there was no need for his help. I didn't want the two of them to meet, as Gage had been texting me and was on his way. It was clear that he wasn't Stephen. After Aaron left, he promised to text me later. About 20 minutes later, Gage arrived just as the nurse was making me walk around before being released. The pain from my recent surgery paled in comparison to the pain in my heart over my love life. But with Gage by my side, his attentive gaze upon me, I couldn't help but feel a sense of peace.

The nurse helped me put on my clothes, and Gage went to get the car. I thought about Gage being repulsed by seeing me so weak. It didn't matter anyway; it was too late; he had already seen me like this. But deep down, I couldn't shake the thought of him being with his ex while I was in such a vulnerable state. All I wanted was for him to hold my hand as we drove home. Despite the pain in my back, my mind was filled with thoughts of Gage's presence again. As he drove me to the pharmacy to pick up my pain medication, I stole glances at him and marveled at this man who consumed my every thought. At a red light, I turned away from him before sneaking another look and catching him smiling at me with his dimples showing. In that moment, all my tension melted away. Why do I love this man so much?

16

After leaving the pharmacy, we pulled up to my house. Gage quickly jumped out of the car and ran over to my door, eager to help me out. As I stepped inside, a wave of nostalgia hit me - this was where it all began. It was here that I first met Gage in person on that late night. I took a seat on the couch, and he asked if there was anything I needed. In my head, I wanted to say, "Only you, you fool". But instead, I simply told him I was fine for now. Gage continued to wait on me hand and foot.

The day quickly turned into night, and Gage decided to stay with me. We both slept on the first floor because I couldn't bear the thought of climbing stairs. It was the first time in a long while that I slept soundly through the night, possibly due to the medication, but I preferred to think it was Gage by my side. The next morning, I woke up to find Gage cooking breakfast for me and taking care of my needs. As I watched this sexy ass man moving around my kitchen, I felt a strong desire to make love to him right there. But then reality hit me - my back is fucked up, and he was back with his ex, even though I still loved him deeply.

He brought me my favorite breakfast and asked if I needed anything else before returning to his man. I wanted him to stay longer but said I was fine. He had an awkward smile and those irresistible dimples. He promised to be there if I needed him and kissed me goodbye before leaving. My soul felt like it left my body as we embraced. I wanted to say "I love you" but kept it inside. Watching him drive away, I felt a gnawing emptiness inside me, like a part of me had left with him. My body suddenly felt heavy and sluggish, as if all the energy had been sucked out of it. Why did he have to go? I couldn't even move without feeling pain in my back, but when he was here, I felt invincible.

17

But then my phone rang, and it was Gage. A spark of happiness lit up inside me and I couldn't help but smile. He always knew how to make me feel better. "Please don't hesitate to call me if you need anything, Chaise. You're not a burden," his words were like a warm hug. And yet, as much as I appreciated his offer, I couldn't shake off the feeling that there was something he wanted to say but didn't. Before I knew it, we were hanging up and I was left alone once again.

As my phone began to ring again, I assumed it was Gage calling me back. But when I checked, it turned out to be Kyra, my best friend. We're so similar that she knows me better than anyone else. Kyra Jane is a stunning 35-year-old woman who is both intelligent and independent, with a curvaceous figure to boot. We've been friends since high school in New Jersey, and somehow, we both ended up living in Atlanta. We hadn't talked in a while because she was dealing with her own issues with her boyfriend Kendrix. There was disappointment evident in my voice, and Kyra immediately sensed that I needed someone to talk to. She also wanted to come by and help me after my surgery. Before I could even explain what happened, she told me she was bringing food from our favorite Mexican restaurant. I adore this woman because I don't have to say anything for her to understand and offer support.

As Kyra pulled up, I realized she already had an extra key to my house, saving me from having to move an inch. My heart jumped as she opened the door, and I couldn't help but smile and tear up at the same time. She joined me on the couch and gave me a warm hug. After some small talk, I finally mustered up the courage to ask her about her relationship with Ken. Her response left me puzzled: "Chaise, this isn't about Ken and me. We're still the same, but he just bores me." She then explained that she came to see me and take care of her twin - our nickname for each other since we think alike and finish each other's sentences. I wanted to focus on her and Ken's issues so I wouldn't have to think about Gage so much. The thought of this whole situation exhausts me. I didn't want to burden Kyra with my problems because it would only add more stress to everything else.

Kyra headed to the kitchen to grab some plates for our Mexican feast. In the meantime, she whipped up some margaritas while I found myself sinking into the couch and opening up about everything that was weighing on me. Kyra sat down next to me, listening intently without even blinking. I could tell she was processing everything because there was a lot to take in. It had been months since we had a real heart-to-heart conversation. When I met Gage, I disappeared into our relationship and lost touch with Kyra. She was going through her own issues with Ken, so we didn't have our usual talks. But now, despite the time apart, it felt like nothing had changed as we caught up with each other's lives.

After she took some time to process what I had just shared, she enveloped me in a tight hug and then headed into the kitchen. As I sat there, feeling emotionally drained, she called out to me from the kitchen, saying that she was making more margaritas because this was going to be a long conversation. Despite taking strong painkillers, I didn't mind indulging in a few drinks - I needed this moment, this session with my best friend. Kyra knew I could handle my alcohol; after all, I am 6'4 and weigh 225 pounds - my body could handle it. She returned with another glass for me, and we continued our heart-to-heart.

Before I knew it, Kyra and I were both a little tipsy and laughing uncontrollably. It had been so long since I had felt this carefree, and it was refreshing. Suddenly, Kyra's phone started ringing and she groaned, knowing it was her boyfriend Ken on the line. She answered reluctantly and I couldn't make out everything that was said, but she told him she was staying the night with me. Ken was familiar with me and didn't mind, but he asked if I needed his help as well. Kyra swiftly declined, saying "No thanks Ken, Chaise and I can handle it." I remarked how kind it was of Ken to help, to which Kyra rolled her eyes and replied, "Don't be fooled, he's just trying to win back my forgiveness. But that's a story for another day."

 I didn't want to pressure Kyra into talking about it, especially since I was enjoying all the attention. We started watching A Thin Line Between Love and Hate and kept the drinks flowing. Before I knew it, we were both asleep, and having someone in the house felt comforting. Sometime during the night, I woke up to see that Kyra was fast asleep next to me. I checked my phone and saw a text from Gage, saying he was just checking up on me. In my tipsy state, I replied that Kyra was with me, but I wished he was there instead. What the hell did I just send him? It must have been the alcohol making me bold. I saw the three dots indicating he was typing a response, but then everything went silent. Oh well, I put my phone down and realized I may have gone overboard once again. The alcohol took control and I fell back asleep.

 I woke up to Kyra getting ready to leave to grab us some breakfast. My mind was consumed with thoughts of the text I sent Gage last night. I grabbed my phone eagerly, hoping to see a response from him. But there were only 10 messages: a few from random guys, one from my mom, and one from Stephen. No reply from Gage, and suddenly I started to panic. Did I say something wrong? As I scrolled through our conversation, I realized that maybe I had gone too far with my last message, even though Gage knows it was nothing compared to what I've said before. I reminded myself that he's in a committed relationship now. The fact that he read my message was enough for me.

  Kyra returned with breakfast in hand, we ate in silence. We were both lost in our own thoughts; mine consumed by a man who wasn't mine, and hers by her complicated situation with Ken. As the day drifted on, we savored each other's company, sharing laughter, tears, and love. But eventually, evening approached, and Kyra had to leave. We said our goodbyes with the promise of seeing each other again soon. As I watched her leave, I was left alone with my thoughts. I knew that my recovery would be a long journey, not just physically for my back, but mentally as well.

  It had been a few weeks since I last heard from Gage, and part of me was relieved. But let's be real - even if he sent a single letter from the alphabet, I'd probably still feel elated. At least I had physical therapy to keep me occupied and help with my fast-healing process; it felt like the surgery never happened. The thought of going back to my life without Gage weighed heavily on me. As a successful writer, I had deadlines to meet for my book and updates to make on social media for my sponsors. It all felt like too much, and I was feeling overwhelmed. How could I write romance novels when I wasn't feeling very romantic myself?

  Dust had started to accumulate on my laptop, a testament to how little I've used it lately. I struggled to come up with ideas, especially anything romantic. Maybe I could write about the pain and struggles I'm currently facing. My agent and manager would probably love the dramatic story as it tends to sell well. But do I really want to share my personal life with the public? Perhaps it could be therapeutic and beneficial to get everything off my chest. For now, I'll shut my laptop and revisit these thoughts after talking with my team.

    The next day I was reminded by my manager that I had an interview coming up. I also had a literary festival to attend as well. I am not ready for either. First thing first, the interview is with Jason Avant. I am not looking forward to this interview not only because of the state of my mind and heart, but because Jason is Aaron's best friend. That's right you read it correctly. He is the best friend of my ex-Aaron. I wanted to cancel but I made this commitment and all the information for the interview has been posted all over Atlanta and on social media. Also, Jason might think I don't want to do it because Aaron is my ex. That's not it at all, I know that Jason can be a little messy. I am thankful for my PR training when I first started my career.

    Jason is known to ask questions that aren't really supposed to be asked. Most people he interviews fold under pressure, but I am determined to keep it together. I know there is a strong chance that Gage will be watching. The show is called Sip with Jason. He and his guests usually sip on tea or wine while being interviewed. You have a choice of sipping on whatever drink it is that you like. But sipping tea is synonymous with gay culture. Jason loves to get all the tea and spill it. I must remember this is for my brand, my previous book and all the things going on with me.

    The interview was coming up, and my doctor had given me the all-clear to resume my normal duties. But what did "normal" even mean for me now? Nothing felt normal anymore. I sat in my Tesla, listening to Beyonce's new album Renaissance, trying to distract myself from the upcoming interview. Suddenly, my phone started ringing with an unfamiliar number. Part of me wanted to ignore it, but I couldn't help hoping that it was Gage calling. When I answered with a smile and excitement in my voice, I was disappointed to hear Jason Avant on the other end. He sounded ecstatic about the interview, but all my enthusiasm disappeared in an instant. I just wanted him to get off the phone so I could be alone with my thoughts.

He was curious about my thoughts on the upcoming interview and expressed his excitement to see me and catch up. My publicist had already spoken with Jason, and they agreed upon the questions that I was comfortable answering, as well as any topics that were off limits - including my dating life (or lack thereof). However, I have a feeling he will still push for answers because that's just his nature. But I am ready for anything he throws my way. Before ending the call, although lying I reassured Jason that I am eager for the interview and can't wait to see him in person.

On the morning of the interview, I received a text from my friends Kyra and Stephen. They reassured me that they would be in the audience, ready to defend me if Jason tried anything. I was grateful for their unwavering support and willingness to stand up for me. When I arrived at the studio lot and parked my car, I took a moment to gather my thoughts. My publicist then called, asking where I was because they were ready for me in my dressing room. As I entered the room, I saw that it had everything I requested, from a margarita to my favorite snacks. It may have been early in the day, but as they say, it's always 5 o'clock somewhere and I needed to relax before the interview.

As I entered the dressing room, my publicist, stylist, and manager all stood up to greet me. I took a seat in front of the mirror and gave myself a quick glance. To be honest, I rarely look at myself in the mirror anymore. But with my team by my side, I knew they would make me look presentable. They always manage to bring back my confidence and make me feel like myself again. A producer from the show then interrupted our preparations, informing us that we were going live in 15 minutes. The nerves kicked in as they always do, but I've learned to embrace them; they keep me on my toes during interviews.

As I walked onstage, I heard the host introduce me "Let's welcome Chaise Kelley." I greeted some of the audience members with handshakes and smiles. Suddenly, I recognized a familiar face in the crowd: it was my ex-boyfriend, Aaron. I wasn't surprised; Jason probably invited him to the show. Despite our past relationship, Aaron and I are still friends, so I approached him and exchanged a handshake. He held on to my hand for longer than necessary, but I managed to free myself and continued walking towards the stage. I hugged Jason before taking a seat in front of the audience. I could feel Aaron's gaze on me like a hawk, but I was determined to give a great interview.

An unsettling thought crossed my mind: what if Gage is watching too? I was more worried about him seeing me than Aaron. My stomach churned with nerves, but I knew I had to be ready for any questions that came my way. Jason began the interview by asking about my previous book and my upcoming one. To my surprise, the audience erupted in applause when my new book was mentioned. After being silent for so long due to my back surgery, I had doubted if anyone still cared about my work. But their reaction made me realize that it was me who had lost interest in myself all this time.

The interview was going smoothly, but I knew Jason had something up his sleeve for the finale. With only seven minutes left, I

24

thought I was in the clear from any awkward questions. But then Jason asked me out of the blue, "So, Chaise, are you seeing anyone at the moment? It's hard to believe that someone like you is single or not dating." I hesitated for a moment but realized that my true feelings would show if I waited too long to answer. I wondered if Aaron had put him up to this. Well, here it goes. "Actually, Jason, I am single and not currently dating anyone. I'm still trying to move on from my previous relationship." The audience gasped, eager for all the details.

As I spoke, I realized that my words were cryptic enough to keep everyone guessing. Jason probably thought I was talking about Aaron and me. And Aaron, well, he believed it was about our relationship. If Gage was watching, he knew the truth. I felt Aaron's eyes on me, hoping for a glimpse into my thoughts. Meanwhile, Jason just wanted me to go into a detailed account of what I said. But I wasn't ready to do that. When Jason asked for an explanation of my last situation, I shot him a look that could kill. "There's no need for explanations," I said firmly, daring anyone to push further. But Jason had to have the last word: "I guess we'll all have to wait for Mr. Kelley's new book to find out."

As I finished the interview, I couldn't wait to escape backstage. Aaron was waiting for me, wanting to talk. The last thing I wanted was a conversation with him. He gave me a concerned look and said, "Hey Chaise, I didn't realize you were still struggling with our breakup. I thought you had moved on. I'm sorry about everything, but if you're willing, I'd like to try working things out." It was sweet of him to think that's what was bothering me - our relationship, our past. But the truth was so far from that. "Thank you, Aaron, but right now I'm focused on myself and we're better off as friends."

25

I could see the disappointment in Aaron's eyes as I gave him my honest response. But even if I wanted to work on our relationship, I couldn't. My heart belonged to another man, a man who ignited a fire within me that Aaron never could. A man who uncovered hidden parts of my soul that I never knew existed. Kyra and Stephen sprang into action, rushing over to offer their support. As they approached, I smiled at them, silently conveying that I was okay. With a subtle glance, I signaled to Kyra that it was time to leave. She and Stephen finished speaking to Aaron before guiding me away from the tense situation. As we left, the weight of the interview lifted off my shoulders and we all breathed a sigh of relief. We headed out to celebrate my successful interview.

We parked our cars and walked into the restaurant together. The hostess immediately recognized me from my recent interview and eagerly gave us the best table available. We took our seats and began catching up. Kyra and Stephen couldn't help but ask about Gage and me. I explained that I hadn't heard from him in weeks. They were both disappointed, but I reminded them that he was in a committed relationship. Deep down, I couldn't help but feel upset too - why weren't Gage and I together? Kyra responded boldly with, "Chaise, forget him and his ugly-ass boyfriend." It was strange because Kyra had never seen a picture of Gage's partner, and I had never mentioned his looks. In my mind, I agreed with her: "Yeah, fuck him and his boyfriend."

Stephen sat quietly because he is over the whole situation, and I am too but it's easier said than done. I just can't erase what Gage and I shared. Stephen was ready for me to move on and see what else was out there. Kyra on the other hand knows me better than anyone and is supportive, although she is pissed about the way Gage handled the whole thing. She really wants me and Gage together because she has never seen me so happy even with Aaron.

As the waiter approached our table to take our drink orders, Kyra and Stephen couldn't help but notice his frequent glances in my direction. I, on the other hand, was too preoccupied with reading the menu and trying to tune out everything around me. Margaritas and shots were ordered as usual. Suddenly, Stephen exclaimed, "Chaise, did you see that gorgeous waiter checking you out? And damn, he's got a nice ass." Irritated, I replied, "No, Stephen. I was too busy trying to decide what to order. So, you two won't complain I'm taking too long." Disappointed, Stephen retorted, "Come on, Chaise. Snap out of it and get in this fine waiter. Get in his ass Chaise, and I do mean ASS!" I gave him a disgusted look while Kyra just laughed at the whole situation. "Stephen," I asked with exasperation, "Do you ever think about anything else besides sex?" Without hesitation, he responded with a chuckle, "Hell NO!"

I excused myself to the restroom, feeling the need to wash my hands and take a moment to look at myself in the mirror. The reflection staring back at me was a mere shadow of who I used to be, but damn, I still looked good. Suddenly, the waiter walked into the bathroom, his smile and gorgeous appearance catching my attention. I couldn't help but notice his toned ass even from the front. He approached me with confidence, pushing me into a stall. In disbelief, I asked him, "What the hell are you doing?" He looked up at me from his position on his knees and explained that my friend Stephen had told him I wanted this, and he wanted me too. As flattered as I was by the waiter's advances after months of being single, I knew we couldn't do this, especially while he was working. So, I stopped him and pulled him up from his knees. "Hey! We can't do this," I said firmly. The waiter licked his lips and responded,

"Okay, playing hard to get? Here, take my number and give me a call sometime. My name is Luke."

Before he left the stall, he kissed me and placed my hands on his plump ass. I couldn't resist enjoying the feeling. I took a few moments to collect myself and calm down before leaving the bathroom. Although I had only been inside for 8 minutes, it felt like an hour had passed. As I exited, Stephen was entering with a smirk on his face. He whispered to me, "You're welcome, Chaise. See you back at the table." Anger boiled up inside me, but I didn't want to cause a scene in front of everyone, so I simply walked back to our table. Once there, I confided everything that happened to Kyra. She could sense my frustration and secretly hoped that I would give in to Luke's advances. She knew that I needed a release from all the pent-up tension and anger building inside me.

Stephen returns to the table, wiping sweat off his face and adjusting his clothes. Kyra was occupied on the phone with her boyfriend Ken, while my attention was focused on Stephen. "So, Stephen, I didn't appreciate you telling Luke to do what he did," I said, trying to sound stern. Stephen just rolled his eyes and responded, "What exactly did Luke do, Chaise?" I couldn't stay mad at Stephen for long, so I laughed and replied, "Nothing really, because I stopped him before he could do anything." It seemed like I had hurt Stephen's feelings because he shook his head and looked down at the menu. After a moment, he looked back up and said, "I just got mine from someone I met on my way to the bathroom, but that's a story for another day." Before I could ask any questions, Luke came over to take our orders with a mischievous look on his face. We placed our orders, and the rest of the night went smoothly without any more surprises.

28

As dinner ended, we all said our goodbyes and went our separate ways. Stephen had plans with a random guy from Jackd, Kyra went home to her partner Ken, and I headed home alone. I resisted the urge to text Luke for a quick session. Arriving home, I found flowers on my doorstep, possibly sent by Gage in guilt after watching my interview. However, they were from Jason and his production team, thanking me for the interview. Disappointed, I left them on the counter and went upstairs to shower and sleep.

The next morning, I woke up to a text from Aaron. I debated whether to respond; on one hand, I didn't want to encourage him, but on the other hand, if I ignored him, he'd probably end up calling me. It's frustrating that Gage doesn't have the same level of concern for me. I don't care about his boyfriend; all I want is for Gage to check on me. But even if I do text him, there's a chance he won't respond, and that would hurt me even more. It's been months since we've spoken, yet my feelings for Gage haven't changed. Despite everything, I still care about him and just want to know how he's doing. I keep telling myself it's better if we don't talk, but who am I kidding? Fuck what's best; I just want to hear from Gage.

After building suspense during the interview with Jason and receiving comments on my IG page, I decided to turn my pain into profit by writing about what I went through with Gage. This could be my best book yet, and it might even be therapeutic for me and others. As I opened a bottle of prosecco to celebrate the moment, I realized this book would practically write itself after my long bout of writer's block. A fire was ignited within me, not the wild passion I had with Gage, but a motivation to write. Writing has saved my life and it's more than just a money maker. I focused on writing, ignoring everything else. Before I knew it, 7PM rolled around and I had 80 pages. The thought of therapy crossed my mind, but I needed this chaos for my new book. I'll seek therapy later, after it's complete. For now, I'm writing raw and hoping for a great payoff.

A couple weeks passed, and I stayed low and didn't go out. I talked to Kyra and Stephen, and they understood. Well Kyra did but Stephen wanted me to go out and get into some shenanigans which in Stephen world means "ass". Stephen kept bringing up Luke and that I should text him. This is the hardest he has ever backed a random. Believe me it must be something in it for Stephen for him to be going this hard. What's in it for him I will figure out later.

As the days passed by in a blur, I came to the realization that this book will require a part two, or possibly even three. My life has been full of unexpected twists and turns, providing me with plenty of material for my writing. It's bittersweet to think about how one man was able to enter my carefully constructed fortress and turn it upside down. I had felt so safe after my break-up with Aaron, but Gage managed to break through my walls and leave me vulnerable once again.

Trapped in my house for weeks on end, I find no desire to venture outside. But at least I have been productive, already reaching chapter 5 of my book. However, as I stare at the screen in front of me, my vision starts to blur, and I realize it's time to give my tired mind a rest. After a long shower, memories come flooding back to me - memories of Gage and our time together in the shower. I remember how I used to massage every inch of his body before we stepped under the warm water. His smile, his touch, his kiss - all of it feels like a distant dream now. As the water cascades down my body, I can almost feel Gage's tongue tracing along my skin once again. How could someone who brought me so much pleasure also brings me so much pain?

30

My hands roamed eagerly over my body, fingers tracing every curve and dip as I moaned loudly, lost in the throes of pleasure. And then, suddenly, I was calling out Gage's name, my voice raw with need and desire. The sensation was intense, almost overwhelming, and I could feel Gage with me in that moment. It was like he was there in the shower with me, his touch igniting sparks of electricity across my skin. My mind raced with fantasies of penetrating him, my grip tight around his neck while he gripped my ass and pulled me deeper inside of him. The water cascading down from the showerhead only heightened our passion, acting as a lubricant for our bodies as we moved together. I couldn't resist biting and kissing his neck as our bodies moved in perfect harmony. And then, just as ecstasy began to wash over me, I cried out Gage's name at the top of my lungs. It felt like my soul was leaving my body as I stood there trembling for what felt like an eternity. If anyone didn't know Gage's name before, they certainly did now after hearing my loud moans for him.

As I stepped out of the shower, my body tingled with a mix of arousal and disbelief. Could it have been real, or was it just my own pent-up desire manifesting itself as a vivid dream of Gage? The memory of our steamy interaction replayed in my mind; each detail etched into my brain like a photograph. It was unlike anything I had ever experienced before, even with all my previous solo escapades. Thinking of him while pleasuring myself brought it to a whole new level, making me feel more alive and connected than ever before.

But as I lay in bed, still processing what had happened, I felt a sense of emptiness as if part of me was missing. I realized that my soul had wandered off in search of Gage, craving more of his touch. It was as if my very being was yearning for him, aching to keep him close and never let go. Fighting to bring myself back to reality, I drifted off to sleep only to wake up to a flood of messages on my phone. My heart skipped a beat when I saw one from Gage among them. My hands trembled as I opened it, afraid that it might all be too good to be true.

But there it was - a simple but significant message from Gage asking if I was free tomorrow night. My mind raced as I tried to process this unexpected turn of events. Without hesitation, I replied eagerly, telling him that I was indeed available. He then shared the details of a dinner reservation he made at one of my favorite restaurants in Atlantic Station at 8PM. My heart leapt with excitement and nerves as I read his message. Was this really happening? Was Gage interested in seeing me again? The thought alone made me excited with anticipation and nervous energy. Tomorrow night couldn't come soon enough.

My mind was a jumbled mess as I received the unexpected news. My thoughts raced, trying to process everything, but it was like my brain had shut down and couldn't form coherent sentences. I wanted to share the news with my friends Kyra and Stephen, but at the same time, I didn't want to get my hopes up in case it turned out to be nothing. Kyra would undoubtedly be ecstatic, but if this fell through, I knew I would feel crushed. And as for Stephen, his negative energy seemed to seep into everything he touched - I didn't want that cloud hovering over this situation.

With no available appointments at my barber's shop, I reluctantly agreed to pay for a home visit tomorrow. But first, I needed something to wear for whatever this occasion may be. Rushing to the mall, I headed straight for my favorite store. The staff greeted me with warm smiles and quickly pulled out several options for me to try on. It felt like they were determined to make sure I left with at least five different outfits, which

32

only added to my confusion about what kind of event this could possibly be. Regardless, I knew I had to pick something that wasn't too over-the-top but would still catch his eye. No, not just catch his eye - I wanted him to be unable to look away from me, specifically my face and my hazel brown eyes that still held so much love for him.

The following day, my barber arrived and rejuvenated me. I checked the time, and it was already 4PM. I had a mere three hours to get ready. Gage sent a text asking if we were still on. Every inch of me wanted to respond with "The fuck! Of course we are, you crazy man!" But instead, I simply replied with "Yes, we're still on, and I can't wait to see you." When Gage reacted to my message with a heart, it brought a smile to my face. He may not be one for expressing his feelings through words, but that simple action showed me that he felt the same excitement. It's still hard for me to believe that after nine long months, I will finally get to see Gage again. So much can happen in nine months; a woman can have a baby in that time. And though I am all man, this situation has been weighing heavily on me and it's time for it to come out. It has reached its full term.

After indulging in a long, hot shower, I carefully selected and put on each of the five outfits I had bought yesterday. With a little creativity, I mixed and matched pieces to create a whole new look. Finally satisfied with my appearance for the night, I took a quick glimpse of myself in the mirror one last time before sending a quick text to Gage to let him know I was on my way. As I made my way towards Atlantic Station, driving down 85 south, excitement bubbled within me. I found a spot to park and sat in my car for a few minutes, taking deep breaths and mentally preparing for the evening ahead. Glancing at the clock, I saw that it was already 7:45PM and realized I needed to head to the restaurant.

Entering the restaurant, I was warmly greeted by the host who led me over to Gage's table. The interior was dimly lit, creating an intimate and cozy atmosphere. The enticing aroma of sizzling steaks and savory sauces wafted through the air as we walked past tables filled with couples laughing and chatting over their meals. As Gage's face broke into a smile, I couldn't help but notice the way his dimples deepened and added to his charm. The host politely pulled out my chair and I sat down, my heart pounding in my chest. My breath was caught in my throat and my thirst seemed to take over me all at once. My dry mouth begged for water, which was already placed on the table before us. But more than that, I craved this man sitting across from me. I wanted to taste him, feel him, and breathe him in.

Our eyes locked in an intense stare, I could barely contain myself as I fought the urge to jump over the table and show him just how much I missed him. Slowly, I repeated a mantra in my head to calm myself down. Before I could even speak, Gage's voice broke through the moment. "Well, hello there Chaise, can I get a hug?" We both stood up eagerly and embraced each other tightly, almost as if we hadn't seen each other in years rather than months. As I hugged him, I couldn't help but notice the familiar scent of his cologne that I loved so much. He remembered.

Finally, we sat back down, and he said, "Thank you for meeting with me Chaise. There's something important I wanted to talk about." My mind raced with anticipation and confusion, but all at once Gage's presence made everything else fade away. His fitted shirt hugged his toned body perfectly, making it hard for me to resist the urge to touch him. And those jeans...I practically had to pry my hands away from wanting to grab his perfect ass. Leaning close to me, he whispered in my ear those three words that sent shivers down my spine: "I missed you." In that moment,

• • •
34

any doubts or worries melted away as I replied with equal fervor, "I missed you too." As we settled back into our seats, Gage's words hung in the air, and I couldn't help but wonder what he wanted to talk about. But for now, all that mattered was being here with him.

CHAPTER 2

Gage sat across from me, his eyes intense and focused as he began to speak. Like a spider in its web, I was poised and ready to catch every word that fell from his lips. "Chaise," he said softly, his voice trembling slightly. "I didn't have the words to say over text, so I thought it was more fitting to meet in person." My heart raced with anticipation as I leaned forward in my chair. "Okay, Gage," I urged him on. "I'm listening." He looked at me with a mixture of hesitation and longing. "Listen, Chaise," he continued, his words slowing and uncertain. "I didn't think you would agree to meet up with me after the way I treated you." Before I could respond, he reached out and placed a finger gently against my lips, silencing me. The simple touch sent shivers down my spine and ignited a familiar fire within me. So, I remained still and allowed him to continue, holding my breath for what he would say next.

"Chaise, I really thought you were going to burst through that door with anger blazing in your eyes. I even had a sinking feeling that you would pour that water on me, as if it could somehow douse the fire between us." If he only knew how desperately I wanted to quench my thirst with that glass of water. I picked it up, finally ready to take a sip, and he jumped. His reaction was almost comical as he flinched away from me, still on edge. He continued, his voice heavy with regret and sincerity, "I owe you an apology for the way I treated you. I disappeared without a word and even though I came back when you had surgery, you deserved so much more than that." I sat there in complete shock, unable to form words as the weight of his long-awaited confession settled upon me. These were the words I had been yearning to hear for so long, and now they were finally being spoken.

36

As Gage spoke, I focused intently on his words, almost seeing them floating around the room. The restaurant was bustling with people, but their noise faded away as I took a few sips of water and listened to him. He looked away for a moment, then back at me, licking his lips. It made me dizzy just being in his presence. He was waiting for my answer, and I was ready to give it. Smiling, I reached out and took his hand in mine. "Gage, I would never pour water on you." My words seemed to surprise him, and I could see the sadness in his eyes as he responded, "I know what I did was wrong...and it hurt you." But before he could explain further, I silenced him with a gentle touch to his lips. "It's okay," I reassured him. "I forgave you a short time ago." His face lit up with relief and he shook his head in amazement. "Chaise, you're unlike any man I've ever met." With a smirk, I replied, "That's because I'm not just any man. And forgiveness is not only for your sake but for my own peace of mind."

The waiter had come by our table at least seven times while we were lost in conversation. Eventually, we ordered some food and drinks, but I wasn't even hungry anymore. Our discussion carried on even after our orders arrived. Four hours flew by, and the restaurant was about to close when Gage and I finally left. We didn't bring up our past relationship or the ex he had left me for. I wanted to ask about him, but I didn't want to ruin the moment. However, his presence here with me suggests he is single now, so maybe I don't need an explanation. Or maybe I do, but I just don't want to ask, so fuck it.

I walked him back to his car and opened his door for him. He smiled at me, happier than ever before. "Chaise, you are always so kind to me. Thank you." I gave him a puzzled look. "Gage, how could I not be kind to you? You're all I ever think about." We hugged tightly and I kissed his forehead because I couldn't handle the intensity of kissing his lips. He got into his brand-new Mustang Mach E, and I shut the door for him. Before he drove off, I made sure to tell him to call or text me when he got home safely. As I was walking back to my car, Gage stopped me and offered to drive me there. My car wasn't parked far, but I saw it as an opportunity for more time with him. He pulled up beside my car and held my face in his hands, leaning in for a kiss.

His kiss was like a bolt of electricity, surging through my body and taking my soul into the stratosphere. It had been far too long since our lips had met, and I couldn't help but revel in the softness of his pink, full mouth against mine. The kiss seemed to last for an eternity, five minutes stretching out into infinity as our bodies pressed together, desperate for more. Finally, I pulled back, my breath ragged and my heart racing. "Gage," I gasped, "we have to stop...I could go on for hours." He grinned at me, his dark eyes sparkling with desire. "Yes, sexy," he said, "I know. Call me when you get home...or I'll call you if I make it there first." As I drove away from him that night, my mind was spinning with all the emotions and thoughts rushing through me. Everything had happened so quickly, like we never stopped talking or being apart. But in that moment, all that mattered was the tingling sensation still lingering on my lips from his unforgettable kiss.

Gage called as soon as I arrived home, letting me know he got there safely and enjoyed our evening together. He even invited me over to his house the next night, which I eagerly accepted. I walked through my front door feeling weightless, almost like my clothes were slipping off me. After a long shower, I climbed into bed and basked in the euphoria of the night. Glancing at my phone, I saw numerous texts and missed calls that I had knowingly silenced during dinner with Gage. At this point whatever I missed will have to wait until tomorrow. All I wanted to do was revel in this moment. I deserved every bit of this feeling. My soul finally returned from the stratosphere, and I slept like a baby. The whole night I dreamed of nothing but making love to Gage repeatedly. I woke up thinking he was next to me. When I realized he wasn't I rushed back to sleep to pick up where my dream had left off.

The following morning, I woke up feeling like a completely different person. After making a nutritious breakfast and hitting the gym, I caught up on all the missed calls and messages. I chatted with Kyra and Stephen, careful not to mention my night with Gage. All I could think about was seeing him again later. Throughout the day, he texted me and expressed his excitement at seeing each other. This wasn't the same reserved Gage I knew before; this one was open and communicative. I was grateful for this newfound connection. Night fell, and it was finally time. I drove to Gage's house, and he was already waiting outside for me.

As I walked into his house, my eyes met his and it was as if time stood still. The intensity in his gaze drew me towards him like a magnet. Without hesitation, we leaned in and our lips melded together in a passionate kiss. Seeking more of his touch, I pulled him closer until our bodies were pressed against each other, every inch of skin tingling with anticipation. The soft melody of Fantasia's "In Deep" filled the air, providing the perfect backdrop for our intimate moment. As we continued to kiss, his hands roamed over my body, leaving a trail of fire in their wake. I could feel the heat building between us as our movements became more urgent.

Suddenly, he took my hand and led me to the center of the living room where we began to sway to the music. It felt like we were in our own little world, lost in each other's embrace. And as we danced, our lips met once again, this time in slow and sensual kisses. In that moment, as I swayed to the slow rhythm of the music with this man in my arms, I felt a sense of weightlessness and complete surrender. It was a feeling unlike any other; one that consumed me entirely, body and soul. Even with Aaron, I had never experienced such intimacy. But in this moment, nothing else mattered except for the two of us and our movements, in perfect unison with each other's desires.

It was a defining moment, one that changed everything between us. And yet it happened so effortlessly, without any discussion or hesitation. Our bodies moved together as if they were meant to be entwined from the start. It was a moment of pure vulnerability, where words were unnecessary, and our souls spoke louder than any conversation ever could. The music of Fantasia served as the backdrop to this pivotal moment, etching it permanently into my memory. This was not mere sex or games; it was a transcendent experience of pure intimacy. Again, my spirit soared high up into the stratosphere, almost as if I were an observer watching our bodies move in perfect harmony. It felt like an out-of-body experience that I never wanted to end.

After the last note of the song faded away, we remained locked in each other's arms. Gage's piercing gaze seemed to penetrate right into my soul, bringing my soul back to my body with a jolt. I returned his intense stare, feeling a rush of emotions and desire coursing through me. His hand brushed against the side of my face, trembling slightly as he looked away. In that moment, I couldn't resist any longer and I took my own hand to turn his face back towards me. Our lips met in a passionate kiss; our bodies pressed tightly together as we both felt our hearts racing with excitement. It was as if our heartbeats were syncing up, forming one powerful rhythm. We paused for a moment to catch our breath and cool down from the intense heat between us.

Gage gently pulled me over to the plush couch, his hands holding mine possessively. I melted into his embrace, my body fitting perfectly against his. He straddled my lap and our lips met in a hungry, fiery kiss. As we deepened the kiss, I ran my hands along his back, feeling every ripple of muscle beneath his shirt. With a mischievous glint in his eyes, Gage lifted his arms and allowed me to remove his shirt. My fingers traced over the defined muscles of his chest and stomach before finding their way to his sensitive nipples. I heard him moaning softly in pleasure as he buried his face in my neck.

"I've missed you so much," I whispered breathlessly, looking into his intense gaze.

"Babe, I missed you too," he replied, before capturing my lips once again.

As we broke away from our passionate embrace, we both realized how famished we were – not just for each other's touch, but for food as well. With a laugh, Gage pulled me by the hand towards his dining room. My bald head was full of sweat, my clothes were disheveled from our intense make-out session, but I didn't care. I was completely intoxicated by this man. Gage guided me to the table, and I sat down, still reeling from the intensity of our moment together. However, my attention quickly turned to the mouth-watering aroma filling the air. To my surprise and delight, Gage had prepared one of my favorite dishes: shrimp alfredo with garlic bread and a fresh salad. I tried to get up and help him with dinner, but Gage wouldn't have it. He insisted on taking care of everything himself, knowing exactly how to cater to me. Finally, he joined me at the table, and we enjoyed a candlelit dinner with Anita Baker's "Sweet Love" playing softly in the background. It was a perfect evening, and I couldn't believe how lucky I was to have Gage by my side.

I wanted to help so I cleared the table and washed the dishes, sounds of Gage's voice called out to me. My heart fluttered in anticipation as I walked into the living room to find him there, looking as radiant as ever. In that moment, time seemed to stand still as I gazed upon his beautiful features. His expression was puzzled, wondering why I had stopped in my tracks. But I couldn't help it - every time I saw him, it was like seeing him for the first time all over again. I wish he could feel the way my heart races and stomach flutters whenever he's nearby. Eventually, I was able to move my legs and feet towards him, drawn like a magnet. He was lying on the couch, engrossed in a movie, but my attention was solely on him. With a gentle touch, I laid down behind him and pulled his body close to mine. Gage turned to look at me, and our eyes locked in an intimate moment. Without hesitation, he leaned in and pressed his lips against mine in a deep kiss. The movie continued in the background, but it didn't matter because before I knew it, we were both fast asleep in each other's arms - the perfect end to a perfect night.

I slowly emerged from my slumber; I saw Gage lying on his stomach before me. The sight of his perfectly round and plump ass caught my attention immediately. I traced the curve of his back with my eyes, marveling at how it seemed to go on forever. My hand instinctively reached out to caress his ass, eliciting a pleasurable moan from him. I couldn't take my eyes off him, like a hawk stalking its prey. My lips followed the trail of my fingers as I made my way down to his ass, pulling down his underwear in one swift motion. And then, without any hesitation, my face dove deep into his ass. I licked, sucked, and kissed every inch of his hole, savoring the intoxicating taste and smell of him. His body jolted with pleasure and his legs began to shiver uncontrollably. His moans grew louder and more desperate with each passing moment. Between licks and kisses, he managed to utter words that sent shivers down my spine: "Ooh shit Chaise, you love my ass, don't you?" With my mouth still full of him, I managed to respond breathlessly: "Hell yeah Gage, I love your ass...I love you." In that moment, nothing else mattered except for the two of us entwined in pure ecstasy.

After all he did for me the night prior, it was now my turn to return the favor and unleash all my pent-up aggression. I eagerly flipped him over onto his back, his body trembling with anticipation. With his legs lifted and spread wide, I dove in to feast on his waiting ass. Gage moaned and gasped as I worked my tongue deep inside him, exploring every inch of his tight entrance. His hands grabbed onto my head, urging me on to go deeper and harder. My own need growing more intense with each passing moment, I couldn't help but push forward with even greater fervor. I wanted Gage to smother me with his body, to consume me entirely. And as he shifted and settled himself onto my face, I eagerly obliged.

The sun's rays were beginning to peek through the windows, signaling the start of a new day. But I was lost in the heat and passion of this moment, unable to tell the time as I continued to devour Gage's body. And then, with a shout that echoed throughout the room, Gage reached his peak and released himself all over my chest. Breathless and completely spent, we collapsed onto the bed in a tangled mess of limbs and sweat. This was a moment of pure bliss, one that I will remember and crave for many nights to come.

43

As we lay together, our bodies still quivering from the intense pleasure we had just shared, Gage and I exchanged a knowing look of satisfaction. Our chests heaved in unison as we caught our breath after such an electrifying experience. But as Gage glanced down at my erection, he noticed that I hadn't ejaculated. I reassured him that it didn't matter, that this was all about him and the emotional connection we share. His satisfaction was my own release. He stared back at me with a mix of surprise and adoration before getting up to retrieve a towel and gently wiping himself off me. Despite wanting to stay in that moment forever, I couldn't deny the primal desires stirring within me. As he headed for the shower, I resisted the urge to text Kyra and reveal Gage's return. This was our secret, at least for now. And as much as I wanted to shout it from the rooftops, I also wanted to savor every moment with Gage without any outside interference or judgment. That's just how much he means to me - enough to make me hold off on sharing our reunion with anyone else for as long as possible.

While Gage indulged in a refreshing shower, I took charge of ordering our breakfast. Cooking has never been my strong suit, but luckily, I knew one of his favorite restaurants that delivered. With Gage's tendency to take long showers, I was confident the food would arrive on time. Just as he stepped out of the bathroom, the doorbell chimed, and our breakfast had arrived. Hurriedly, I arranged the plates and utensils on the table, trying to make it look like a homemade meal. Seeing the spread in front of him, Gage's face lit up with joy. "You ordered from my favorite spot!" he exclaimed, making me feel accomplished. Grinning back at him, I replied, "Anything for you, Gage. The aroma of freshly cooked food filled the room as we sat down to enjoy our meal together.

44

Gage was happily devouring his breakfast while I excused myself to take a shower. Standing under the warm spray, my mind reeled as I tried to process everything that had happened between us. A part of me didn't want this moment to end, but I knew I had responsibilities at home. My book deadline was looming, and I only had two weeks left to submit it. Lost in thought, I suddenly felt a hand on my back - Gage's hand. He told me he understood my need to leave and finish my work, but then he leaned in close, his pink lips slightly parted. "Not so fast, handsome," he said seductively, "let me help you with something." And before I could protest, his expert hand was wrapped around my length and his mouth was on mine. Our eyes locked in a hypnotic gaze as our bodies moved in unison, my soul soaring once again under Gage's touch.

I was completely consumed by Gage's touch, my body yearning to stay in his embrace. With Gage, penetrating him wasn't even necessary; just a simple touch, a piercing gaze, a fiery kiss or an enthralling conversation was enough to make me come in every way. As I felt myself on the verge of climaxing, Gage suddenly dropped to his knees in front of me. It all happened so quickly that before I could even comprehend what was happening, I exploded in ecstasy into Gage's mouth. When he stood up, I couldn't help but search for any remnants of my release, only to find that Gage had devoured every drop. My soul felt like it was floating in pure bliss, and I couldn't resist passionately kissing him and holding him close. I wanted to taste what he tasted. Yeah, I know I'm a freak! In that moment, all I wanted was to stay in Gage's arms forever.

After I finished my refreshing shower, I slipped into my clothes from the night prior and headed out to the living room where Gage was engrossed in the TV. He looked up as I approached and walked me to the door, his hand warm against mine. We embraced tightly, our lips meeting in a passionate kiss that lasted for five indulgent minutes. When we finally broke apart, I felt like I was floating on a cloud. My heart was still at Gage's house, lingering in the warmth of his embrace. As I made my way to my car, I couldn't remember the drive home - my mind was lost in a state of euphoria. Even as I settled into bed that night, my soul still felt connected to Gage's. I called him to let him know I arrived safely, but just wanted an excuse to hear his voice again. With renewed energy and inspiration, I sat down at my laptop to work on my book. It will no longer be a book of pain but ecstasy. I deleted the work I already typed. Gage's presence had added a spark to my creativity, igniting a fire within me that caused the words to flow effortlessly from my fingertips onto the screen in front of me.

The blanket of night descended; I welcomed the promise of sleep. My body hummed with a sense of accomplishment not only from my time spent with Gage but also from the progress I had made on my book. It all felt like a surreal dream, and yet here I was living it. Excitement brimmed within me as I spoke with Kyra, still holding back some details for fear of jinxing it all. Then, before retiring for the night, I made sure to speak with Gage and wish him a goodnight. Soon, a deep and peaceful slumber overtook me, preparing me for what lay ahead. The next morning dawned bright and full of promise. After a refreshing shower, I practically ran to my laptop, eager to continue where I left off. With determination in my heart and the words flowing effortlessly from my fingertips, I just knew today would be the day I finished my book. In fact, I even came up with a title that felt perfect: LOVE - simple yet powerful, just like the story it held within its pages.

As the final words of my book fell into place, I felt an immense sense of relief wash over me. But as soon as I closed the cover, my phone rang, and Stephen's name flashed on the screen. We made plans to meet for lunch at a restaurant in Dunwoody, our usual spot for catching up. Our conversation danced around everything except Gage, the one person I desperately needed to talk about but couldn't bring myself to. I drove home, a nagging feeling settled in my stomach. It had been hours since I finished my book and still no word from Gage. My worries grew with each passing minute until I finally picked up my phone and called him. Straight to voicemail. Panic began to bubble inside me, fueled by memories of past experiences with Gage. Frantically pacing back and forth, my mind raced alongside my heart.

Just when I thought I couldn't take it any longer, a text from Gage appeared on my screen: "Sorry...". Without hesitation, I dialed his number again, only to be met with another voicemail. My fingers shook as I typed out a pleading response but received no reply. Fear and frustration consumed me as I waited for any sign of life from Gage. What in the actual fuck! My heart was pounding, my palms were sweaty, and I could feel panic rising within me. This couldn't happen again. I collapsed onto the nearest chair, trying to catch my breath. But then I stood up abruptly, grabbed my car keys, and headed out the door. I refused to let this be a repeat of the first time it happened.

I drove in a frenzy to Gage's house, memories flooding back with each turn of the wheel. As I pulled up to the familiar driveway, there was an eerie stillness in the air. No lights on, no signs of life inside. I hesitantly knocked on the door and rang the doorbell, but there was no answer. My heart sank as I realized he wasn't home. Feeling defeated, I retreated to my car and waited for what felt like hours. The weight of the situation was suffocating me, making it hard to breathe. And as the minutes ticked by, anxiety turned into anger and frustration. I couldn't just sit here and do nothing.

With shaky hands, I gripped the steering wheel and drove back home. My mind was a whirlwind of emotions - confusion, regret, and anger - all fueled by the concoction of different liquors from my bar cart that I had hastily mixed. The burning sensation in my throat matched the fire that raged within me. How could I have let this happen again? The guilt and shame weighed heavy on my chest as I tried to make sense of it all. But for now, all I could do was drown my sorrows in another drink and hope that somehow things would work out for the best

As I lay in bed, my mind was racing with thoughts of Gage. I had tossed and turned all night, unable to find any peace or slumber. The sun was slowly creeping up into the sky, a stark reminder that I hadn't slept at all. My phone taunted me with its silence - no messages from Gage. I couldn't help but blame myself for letting him back into my life so easily. Why didn't I ask more questions during our dinner? I knew it was a defense mechanism - not wanting to know the truth about his past with his ex. And now, as I thought back on my visit to his house, I realized I had never really looked around. My rose-colored glasses had blinded me to any signs of a current relationship. Twenty-four hours ago, everything seemed so perfect. Now, all I could focus on was his one-word reply: "Sorry...". What did that even mean? Was he truly sorry, or just a sorry excuse for a fucking man?

The shrill ring of my phone pierced through the quiet room, causing me to rush towards it with a mix of hope and anxiety. I desperately wanted it to be Gage on the other end, offering an apology for all the chaos he had caused. But as I answered the call, a voice answered

48

back that was not Gage. It was from the management company representing me, informing me that my previous manager was no longer with them and that a new one had been assigned. The name of this new manager was Summer, and her reputation preceded her. I had heard stories about her from other clients she represented - how she was ruthless in getting the best for her clients, never settling for anything less. She was known for going above and beyond for them, making sure they were always taken care of and never screwed over. With a mix of apprehension and curiosity, I awaited my first interaction with Summer as my new manager.

As my call with my management company ended, a new one lit up my phone. I was surprised to hear the voice of Summer on the other end. Her enthusiasm radiated through the receiver, and we ended up talking for over an hour. It was then that I learned she had always dreamed of representing me. For a moment, the excitement of working with Summer made me forget all about Gage and his betrayal. But as we discussed my upcoming book release, the memories came crashing back with a force that knocked the breath out of me. Suddenly, I couldn't fathom releasing this book or facing the public eye again. Summer sensed my hesitation and confusion, prompting me to blurt out everything that had been weighing on me. She listened patiently, offering words of comfort and understanding. In that moment, it felt like a weight had been lifted off my shoulders as Summer became someone I could confide in without any personal ties or judgment. Apologizing for dumping all of this on her, she simply laughed it off and reassured me that she was here to support me no matter what.

A heavy silence hung in the air for what felt like an eternity before Summer finally broke it with a sharp, "So Chaise, what the fuck are you going to do?" The words hit me like a slap in the face, jolting me out of my thoughts. I sat there, stunned, as she continued to talk. Her voice was urgent and determined, reminding me of my looming deadline and the weight of expectations resting on my shoulders. She knew that the world was waiting for my book, and she was not about to let me waste any more time feeling sorry for myself. She demanded that I meet her at her sleek Midtown Atlanta office within the next hour. As I hurried to gather my things and make my way to her, I couldn't help but feel a mix of excitement and dread at what this meeting could mean for my future.

I entered Summer's office; my eyes were immediately drawn to her stunning beauty. She had an air of confidence and power that radiated from her as she sat behind her desk. The stories of her ruthlessness were overshadowed by the sight of her captivating features. I took a seat in front of her, clutching my laptop tightly. She stared at me with piercing eyes, seemingly trying to read my thoughts. "So, Mr. Chaise Kelley, we need to get this book out," she stated firmly. My heart sank as I replied, "I can't release something that I no longer believe in." Summer's response was quick and decisive, "Then write something that you do believe in. You still have a week, and I know you can do it." Her words ignited a fire within me. The anger and frustration I had been holding onto needed an outlet. In that moment, I made the decision to rewrite my book yet again from scratch, pouring my soul into every word.

Before I left Summer's office, she told me that I had a new friend in her. I knew she meant it. It was unusual for her to befriend a client, but I needed her new friendship. I needed new eyes on the situation. I knew Summer was going to have her foot on my neck and wasn't going to let me fail. I wasn't going to let me fail. When I arrived home, I went to work. Fuck love, fuck being hopeful, fuck apologies, fuck it all. I was on a rampage and my book titled LOVE will now be titled LIAR. I stayed up all night writing. I fell asleep at my desk and woke up and started writing again. I'm going to let the world know my hurt, my rage, my confusion. Two days had passed, and I was glued to my laptop. The book was finished and ready to be submitted. I sent the manuscript to Summer.

After what felt like forever, Summer finally called me. Her voice was filled with excitement and admiration as she exclaimed, "Brilliant!" I was taken aback by her reaction because this book was the rawest and most vulnerable piece of writing I had ever produced. It was dark, full of pain, and a departure from my usual romantic works. I couldn't help but feel nervous yet empowered by this new direction in my writing. As I closed the chapter on both the book and my chaotic relationship with Gage, I was determined to leave behind all the hurt and avoid falling back into the depression I suffered through the first time around. Hearing Summer's rave review of my book gave me a much-needed boost of confidence and validation. With her support, there was nothing left for me to do but sit back and let her handle all the final details for publishing. I knew that with Summer on board, my book would soon reach its intended audience and make its mark in the literary world.

I purchased a patio set that ended up being just for show. But one night, I decided to use it and sat outside in my backyard. As I lay in my hammock, I gazed up at the stars on a warm summer evening and pondered over the chaotic mess that was my life. Will my new book be well-received? Will my readers appreciate the change in direction? And most importantly, will Gage ever reach out to me again? So many uncertainties lingered in my mind. Despite everything, I still harbored feelings for Gage and longed to hear from him. In that tranquil moment under the night sky, I finally felt my body relax as I exhaled all my pain and worries into the universe.

This moment is crucial, and I must maintain complete focus. In just a short while, my book will be released to the world, and with it comes a whirlwind of interviews and book signings. I cannot allow my emotions to overpower me, although every fiber of my being longs to collapse and surrender. Trembling, I returned inside my home, stripped off my clothes in a daze, and let the hot water from the shower soak into my skin. Exhaustion weighed heavy on my mind and body, threatening to pull me under. But I forced myself to climb into bed, praying for a better day to come tomorrow. In the silence of the night, my thoughts swirled like a tempestuous storm, unable to find peace even in sleep.

Two months had passed in the blink of an eye. My book had taken off, soaring to the top of best-seller lists, thanks in part to Summer's expert PR skills. The media blitz was non-stop, with interviews, signings, and appearances filling up my calendar. Yet amidst all the chaos and excitement, I still hadn't told Kyra or Stephen about Gage. A part of me felt like it was for the best, that it was easier to just let him fade into a distant memory. But another part of me couldn't shake the feeling that it was all just a dream, a figment of my imagination. Despite the success of my book, I couldn't help but feel a sense of sadness knowing that it was mainly about a man who had ghosted me not once, but twice. It was bittersweet - turning my pain into power and money. Sometimes I felt invincible, riding high on my accomplishments, but other times I felt completely powerless and small. All I wanted was to know if Gage was okay. Why did I still care so much about someone who clearly didn't give one fuck about me? The thought plagued me constantly as I navigated the highs and lows of renewed fame.

52

My ex, Aaron, was incredibly supportive of my latest release. I'm grateful for his friendship and the fact that we can still share moments like celebrating over dinner. During our catch-up, he opened up about his own romantic life, and I couldn't help but reciprocate by telling him all about Gage. To my surprise, Aaron remained supportive and only wanted to see me happy. It's funny because I had promised myself never to mention someone I was dating to Aaron, yet here I am doing the opposite - and it feels liberating. For a moment, I felt myself reconnecting with Aaron.

I considered taking Aaron back to my place, but I couldn't shake the nagging doubts. Was I just being weak in the moment? Would this ruin our friendship or confuse us both? These were the thoughts running through my head as we talked. Aaron had recently ended a relationship and I was still hung up on Gage. It wouldn't be fair to him or me to act on our physical attraction. When I brought it up, Aaron agreed that it wasn't the right choice. We both knew there could be consequences if we gave in to our desires.

After saying goodbye to Aaron, I made my way back home. It was a relief to know that despite all the challenges we faced, Aaron and I could still be there for each other. I was surprised by how easily I opened up to him about another man in my life. I had always avoided discussing our love lives in the past, but maybe it was because I still harbored feelings for Aaron deep down. Even though we ended things amicably, it was still difficult because we wanted different things and mutually decided to go our separate ways.

I pulled into my garage; and a sleek, electric blue Tesla pulled into my driveway. A familiar feeling of excitement swelled within me as I remembered the meeting I had scheduled with Summer. She and I had formed a strong bond and were now best friends, no longer just manager and client. As we saw each other, we both rushed into a hug, a bottle of wine and a basket of gourmet goodies in her arms. We settled in on my cozy couch, surrounded by the smell of warm vanilla scented candles and soft jazz playing in the background. Our conversation covered everything from our upcoming projects to our personal dating lives. Summer gushed about her new man; a successful real estate mogul who seemed to make her radiate with happiness. It was heartwarming to see her so content, knowing she deserved every bit of joy in the world. As we discussed our busy schedules ahead, I couldn't help but feel grateful for our friendship and all the support we gave each other in this hectic industry.

Our meeting ended; I couldn't help but feel a twinge of jealousy as Summer excitedly mentioned her plans with her man. As she drove off, the emptiness of another night alone settled in. Memories of Luke, the charming waiter I had met a while ago, resurfaced in my mind. It had been ages since we last spoke, ever since that encounter in the restaurant bathroom. Now, on a whim, I impulsively decided to reach out to him. Surprisingly, he responded immediately and eagerly accepted my invitation to come over.

Luke's car pulled up in my driveway. We didn't exchange any words; we both knew what he was there for. In that moment, all I wanted was an escape from my thoughts, an escape from the loneliness that had consumed me. Luke understood this and let me use him however I pleased. But even after our passionate encounter, I still felt hollow inside. As soon as it was over, Luke left without a word, leaving me alone once again. It hit me then, how low I had stooped to satisfy my physical desires and numb my emotional pain. Is this what love has reduced me to? Am I failing at love or is it failing me? I have always been faithful to love, but now lust seems to be the one winning. And I can't shake off this unsettling feeling of emptiness.

The moon hung low in the sky, casting a soft glow on the city below as I sat on my patio, phone in hand. I took a deep breath before dialing Kyra's number, anxious to hear her voice and catch up on all that had been happening while we were both caught up in our hectic lives. As she updated me on her dealings, I couldn't help but feel sadness for the strained relationship she was going through with Ken. It was almost comical how we were both entangled in these crazy situations, yet still managed to find solace in each other's company.

I hesitated for a moment, questioning whether I should tell her about my own troubles. But then I remembered why Kyra was my best friend - because she always listened without judgment and offered support and understanding. So, I finally came clean, revealing everything that had been weighing on my mind and heart. To my surprise, Kyra didn't get upset or angry, but rather expressed disappointment that I had kept it all inside for so long. But that was just like Kyra - always putting others before herself. She had probably known something was wrong all along, especially after reading my latest book which delved into some of my personal struggles. In a way, it felt good to confide in her, to have someone who knew me so well and accepted me unconditionally.

Our conversation continued late into the night, the distant sounds of the city faded away and it felt like it was just me and Kyra catching up on lost time. The cool breeze brushed against my skin and the stars twinkled above us as we laughed, reminisced, and supported each other. Despite the challenges we were both facing, being able to reconnect with my bestie made everything seem a little less daunting.

55

As I flipped through my packed calendar, a sinking feeling settled into my chest. My schedule for the summer was jam-packed and there seemed to be no room for anything else, not even spending time with my friends. A book tour awaited me, both internationally and in the states. While part of me wanted to cancel it all, I knew that once I made a commitment, I would stick to it. After a long shower, I finally collapsed into bed, knowing that soon I would have to pack and prepare myself to put on an act and become the famous author, Chaise Kelley. Many would say I am blessed with this opportunity, and I am grateful, but it is far from easy. The money and success are great, but without Gage by my side to share it with, it feels incomplete.

I won't bore you with the mundane details of my book tour, so let's fast forward. The seasons passed by in a blur - summer, fall, winter - as I traveled from city to city. By the time I arrived back home in Atlanta, everything looked brand new - even my house. Though I had the option to return home during my few days off, I purposely stayed away. Being on the road helped clear my mind and escape any reminders of what I left behind. The tour did more than just boost my brand and finances - it also gave me a newfound perspective on life. Despite the exhaustion from endless signings and interviews, I felt rejuvenated and ready to tackle whatever came next.

Exhausted from a long day, I collapsed onto my couch as soon as I got home. Just as I was drifting off to sleep, my phone rang, and Stephen's name appeared on the screen. He wanted to come over and talk. I hesitated, unsure if I had the energy for a conversation, but ultimately agreed to let him come over. When Stephen arrived, he wasted no time in blurting out his plan: "Chaise, we are going on a vacation!" My tired mind struggled to process this sudden announcement. Didn't he realize I had just returned from a trip? But Stephen seemed unbothered by my exhaustion or recent travels. This would be his treat and I could choose the destination. Memories flooded my mind of people talking about Guam. It wasn't until now that I considered going there. Without much thought, I blurted out "Guam" as my chosen destination.

I made the decision to visit Guam and see what all the talk was about. When I mentioned Guam to Stephen, he immediately became excited. It was obvious that he knew someone there. "Let me guess, you have a connection there?" I asked him playfully. He rolled his eyes and responded, "Just because you're my best friend doesn't mean you know everything." As I walked towards the kitchen, I couldn't resist asking, "So what's this guy's name?" Stephen burst out laughing, "You're an asshole, Chaise. But his name is Jaden and he's in the military."

Stephen began to tell me the story of how he and Jaden had a long-distance relationship that didn't work out. He still missed Jaden dearly but saw it as fate that they were not meant to be together. Unlike Stephen, who never seems to get attached, I secretly yearned for an attachment with someone. However, I couldn't fully commit because my heart was still tied to Gage. I chose the dates and Stephen handled the rest. It's crazy to think that in just 15 days, I'll be in Guam. After all I've been through, I deserve this vacation more than anything.

The absence of one person was starkly noticeable on this getaway: Kyra. As the next day dawned, I called her, hoping she could join us. But my hopes were dashed as she explained that she couldn't make it due to ongoing issues with Kendrix. Honestly, a part of me was relieved at the thought of them breaking up. Lately, I had noticed a change in Kyra - a sadness and heaviness that seemed to weigh her down. It pained me to see her like this, knowing that her relationship was the cause. Selfishly, I longed for her to be free from the burden. Kendrix was constantly irritating me, even though he wasn't my man or my problem to deal with. Damn fuck Gage, fuck Kendrix, fuck them all! When I return home, I'll have to check in with Kyra and see where she and Ken stand.

In the days leading up to my trip, I made a promise to pamper myself. These last few months have been a tumultuous rollercoaster of highs and lows. The chaos and uncertainty have taken their toll on me, but now it's time to let it all go. With a deep breath, I release all the negativity and bad energy out into the universe. From this moment forward, I am surrendering everything to God. I am determined to break free from anything that has been holding me back before embarking on my journey. I know that I deserve so much more than what I have settled for in the past. As night fell, I found myself sitting on my couch, journal in hand, pouring my thoughts onto the pages. Writing has always been my therapy and source of strength during tough times.

With each passing day, I felt a sense of freedom from the emotional hold that Gage had over me. The once suffocating grip was now loosening its grasp and the feeling was exhilarating. Bit by bit, the tight grip I had on myself was fading away as well. I couldn't believe how deeply I had allowed myself to become entangled with the same man, for the second time around. But from this moment onward, I decided to be selfish with my own needs and desires - my time, my love, my essence. Love had consumed me and blinded my judgement, but now it was time to look towards the future and acknowledge all that I have to offer. As I repeated these affirmations to myself, a fire began to ignite within me - not the fiery passion I once held for Gage, but a new flame burning for my own personal growth and self-love. I knew that true love would come when I was truly ready for it.

The day of the much-anticipated trip had arrived in a whirlwind. Stephen and I met at the bustling Atlanta Airport, greeted by the rushing sound of overhead announcements and the rush of people hurrying to their gates. As we boarded our flight, my heart raced with excitement. To my delight, Stephen had surprised me with first class tickets, and I couldn't help but feel like I was floating on cloud nine. Our journey would involve two flights, as there was no direct route to Guam. With each passing mile, I could feel the anticipation building within me.

Our first flight took us from Atlanta to Honolulu, the warm Hawaiian sun greeting us as we stepped off the plane for a brief layover. The vibrant colors and soothing tropical scents filled my senses, making it hard to leave this paradise behind. But soon enough, we were back on board our second flight to Guam. I couldn't help but notice that Stephen's mind seemed preoccupied with thoughts of Jaden. He politely brushed off any attempts by the attractive male flight attendants to catch his attention, clearly focused on our destination. And as we finally landed in Guam, I stepped off the plane and felt like I had been transported to another world - a dreamy paradise filled with sandy beaches and crystal-clear waters.

CHAPTER 3

With a flourish, Stephen arranged for a luxurious car service to pick us up from the airport and whisk us away to our hotel. As we drove through the winding roads of Guam, I couldn't help but be mesmerized by the breathtaking views of the ocean and lush green land. It was a hidden paradise that I couldn't wait to explore. Our hotel was no exception - a stunning oasis nestled in the heart of this forgotten gem. As we checked into our adjoining suites, I couldn't contain my excitement. This was going to be the perfect getaway. After taking some time to settle in and freshen up, I stepped out onto my balcony. The warm tropical breeze caressed my skin as I took in the panoramic views of the island. It was like something out of a dream.

I reached for my phone and opened Instagram, eager to share this magical moment with my followers. It had been too long since I last posted, and I made a mental note to engage more with my audience during this trip. After all, what better way to spread the word about this enchanting destination than through social media? With my phone in hand, I captured the beauty of my surroundings and took a few selfies to remember the moment. Excited to share my experiences, I quickly posted the pictures on my Instagram account before meeting up with Stephen for some much-needed sustenance. We ventured to a popular restaurant, its warm lights and inviting aromas drawing us in. As we sat and talked for hours, indulging in delicious food and refreshing drinks, it felt like time stood still. Stephen was visibly jittery about seeing Jaden tonight, but I reassured him and encouraged him to have the time of his life. After our satisfying lunch, we strolled down to the beach to unwind and continue our indulgence in more drinks. Seeing me finally relax and smile brought joy to Stephen's face.

As Stephen and I laid on the beach, basking in the warm sun and cool breeze, a sense of peace overtook me. I closed my eyes and let out a deep breath, feeling my whole-body sink into the soft sand beneath me. Stephen had brought an array of delicious drinks and as I sipped on them, a fleeting thought of Gage crossed my mind. My body responded with a surge of desire, and I quickly had to roll onto my stomach to hide my dick print from Stephen and the other people on the beach. "Let me focus on something else," I thought to myself as I asked Stephen to pass me another drink. The combination of the gentle lull of the waves and the alcohol began to make me feel drowsy. As I drifted off to sleep, I knew that this quiet moment with Stephen was exactly what I needed to escape from any thoughts or worries about Gage.

After I awoke, we both retreated to our separate rooms to prepare for the night ahead. Our main destination was the island's most popular gay club - an absolute must-visit spot. I was eager to let myself go and perhaps even bring someone back to my room. Stephen couldn't contain his excitement at seeing this wild side of me come out. Ever since Gage, I had been holding back and still acting as if I were in a committed relationship. But Stephen wanted me to embrace the free-spirited nature of the island and indulge in all it had to offer. I knew that Jaden would be joining us later, making it a fun-filled group outing. As for behavior, Stephen would be at his best behavior because of Jaden while I threw caution to the wind and behaved like I had no sense of manners or etiquette. The thought alone made me anticipate the night ahead.

I watched Stephen frantically change outfits seven times in preparation for his meet with Jaden. I had never seen him so excited about a man before. It reminded me of how I used to feel when I was getting ready to see Gage. But that was all in the past now, and I couldn't be happier for my friend. I hoped that this time, Jaden would be the one for him, because I was tired of seeing Stephen bounce from guy to guy. I wanted to show him that true love is worth it, although lately I've been questioning if it's possible for me in my own love life.

I left Stephen to finish getting ready and went to get dressed myself. Tonight, I'll be in the corner with some random guy's ass pressing on me. It's funny how things have changed; I used to judge Stephen for being promiscuous, and now here I am, roaming around looking for a stranger to make me feel good. But it's my vacation, and tonight is the night that I let loose and seek some attention from someone new. Fate, please be on my side tonight because I really need this.

After a couple of hours, I joined Stephen and Jaden downstairs. I couldn't help but notice how stunning Jaden was, and it was clear that Stephen was absolutely smitten with him. It had been a while since I'd seen him so happy. Stephen introduced me to Jaden, and we all headed to the club together. I was dressed in all black, with a revealing shirt that left little to the imagination. I wasn't messing around tonight; my goal was to leave with some numbers or maybe even someone. As soon as we stepped into the club, it was packed with people. We made our way through the different rooms until we found one with music and an ambiance that suited us.

When I approached the bar, both bartenders quickly recognized me. To my surprise, I was not charged for a single drink and decided to leave a generous tip in return. As I sipped on my drink, I noticed Stephen and Jaden sitting at a nearby table. I made sure they had drinks as well before heading to the dance floor where the music was pulsing. The beat was infectious, and I couldn't resist moving my body to it. It didn't matter if I danced alone or with someone else; all that mattered was letting loose and forgetting my worries. Suddenly, I caught a glimpse of Stephen and Jaden dancing provocatively together. I jokingly yelled at them to "GET A ROOM!" which they found hilarious as they continued to move their bodies sensually.

As I turned my head to the right, a figure caught my eye. It was like a magnet, pulling me towards it. With a double take, I couldn't believe what I saw. This man was stunningly beautiful and stood out from the crowd effortlessly. My eyes must be playing tricks on me, I thought as I rubbed them in disbelief. But no, there he was - someone very familiar to me. Moving closer to get a better look at this breathtaking vision before me, I stopped suddenly in my tracks. Could it really be him? A jolt of excitement ran through me as I felt my heart race and my dick responded to his presence. It had to be him - Gage, my fucking ex. But wait...who was this man dancing intimately with him? The shock and confusion overwhelmed me as I tried to make sense of the situation. Is this really Gage or did he have an identical twin that I didn't know about? My mind raced as I struggled to process what was happening before me - Gage, the love of my life, dancing with another man.

I stood frozen, a statue amid the pulsing crowd. The music pounded through my body, but my attention was solely on Gage. His moves were fluid and mesmerizing, sending an electric current straight to my core. Suddenly, a random began dancing on me, mistaking my hard dick for interest in him. I pushed him away like move bitch, my eyes never leaving Gage. Suddenly Gage noticed me, and he stood there like a statue himself, as if he had seen a ghost. Well call me Casper because I'm here. The man dancing with Gage looked puzzled as to why he had suddenly stopped dancing. It was as if we were both drawn to each other by an invisible force, floating through the throngs of people until we were face to face. The magnetic pull between us was undeniable, and I couldn't resist the pull any longer.

As if in a trance, I found myself standing face to face with Gage. His breath was heavy and hot against my skin, the result of dancing with another man who followed closely behind him like a loyal puppy. In that moment, the rest of the party seemed to fade away as Gage's voice cut through the music. "Well, well, well, look at who it is," he said, his eyes locked on mine. My heart clenched with anger and frustration, but I kept my composure and replied coolly, "In the flesh, Gage." The man next to him shifted uncomfortably, his eyes burning into me like a hawk watching its prey. I wanted to ask who he was and tell him to go play in traffic or dance with someone else, but I held my tongue hoping it could be in Gage ass later. I didn't want to ruin the moment.

Gage broke our intense eye contact and questioned, "Chaise, what are you doing here?" I retorted with a raised eyebrow, "I could ask you the same thing, stranger." Gage suggested that we step outside to talk because the music was overwhelming, and his little puppy (dance partner) looked annoyed. He excused himself from the guy he was talking to and motioned for me to follow him. I didn't bother telling Stephen where I was going; he seemed too occupied with Jaden anyway.

As we stepped outside, my pulse raced, and my palms grew clammy. I had so much to say to Gage, but all that came out was a

64

jumbled mess of anger and confusion. "Why the hell did you disappear on me...again?" I demanded, my voice trembling with emotion. Gage's face contorted as he searched for the right words to explain himself. But I didn't care about his excuses, I needed answers. "Tell me why you're here and who the fuck was that guy you were dancing with," I spat out, my voice rising in frustration. He seemed annoyed by my questions, but I couldn't back down now. For too long, I tiptoed around our issues to avoid conflict, but not anymore. I needed to know the truth, even if it hurt more than his abandonment ever could.

Chaise, I know I owe you an explanation, but please, just listen. Gage's words spilled out in a jumbled rush, tumbling over one another as he desperately tried to convey what was on his mind. "I am so sorry for everything that I did and did not do," he said, his voice cracking with emotion. But then, the next thing he said cut me like a knife. "Chaise, the man I was dancing with is my fiancé." My heart stopped in my chest as realization dawned on me. I couldn't even process what he was saying before the anger flooded through me. "That's your fiancé?" I yelled; my voice could be heard by people passing by, I'm sure. "You're telling me that's your fucking fiancé? What are you even saying to me right now, Gage? Because none of this makes sense!" The air between us crackled with tension as our words hung suspended in the night sky

Gage's expression changed, showing surprise and shock, as I made the decision to stand up for myself. He grabbed my hands, trying to calm me down. I couldn't deny that his touch sent a jolt of electricity through me. Slowly, I started to relax under Gage's touch. "Listen, Chaise," he said softly. "There's a lot that has happened, and I knew my fiancé before I ever met you. And no, it wasn't my ex that I left you for." His words hit me like a double blow to the chest. He had known this other guy while we were together. As my anger turned to hurt, I began to pull away from him. But Gage refused to let go of my hand, and the longer he held on, the more hurt I felt.

 Just as we were about to speak, Gage's fiancé emerged from the building and saw us. I quickly pulled my hands away from Gage's grasp and walked away, not wanting to deal with any potential awkwardness. Gage called out my name, but I didn't look back. It felt like if I did, I would turn into a statue. I kept walking for what seemed like hours, ignoring the calls and texts from Stephen who was probably worried about my sudden disappearance. He knew I wouldn't just leave without telling him first.

 My phone buzzed in my hand, and I saw Gage's name appear on the screen. I ignored the call and continued walking, trying to clear my mind. A few moments later, a text from Gage popped up, saying that we needed to talk. I rolled my eyes, thinking to myself that there was nothing left to talk about since he had already made his decision. How did my dream vacation turn into such a nightmare? Lost in thought, I arrived back at the hotel and realized that I was no longer drunk from earlier. The shock of Gage's announcement had sobered me up quickly. Stripping off my clothes, I noticed that my arousal was still present, a reminder of how easily my body responded to Gage despite being angry with him. Apparently, my brain hadn't sent the message to my dick yet about how pissed off I was at him.

 Lying in bed, I texted Stephen to let him know that I was fine, but I needed some time alone. I didn't bother to check if he replied because before I knew it, sleep had overtaken me, and I was probably snoring. When I woke up the next morning, I saw a few texts from Stephen asking what was going on. Then, I noticed one from Gage as well, asking to talk. The urge to call him and see what he had to say was too strong to resist. So, I reached for my phone and dialed Gage's number.

Gage's voice on the phone still had the power to make my body flush with desire, despite the anger I felt towards him. How was it possible to be both aroused and furious at the same time? Gage spoke first, acknowledging my right to feel hurt and angry. He also understood if I wanted to walk away forever. But before I did that, he asked if we could have dinner tonight. He knew it was a big request, but it meant a lot to him to see me one more time.

Defeated and powerless against his manipulative charm, I reluctantly gave in to meeting up with him. But my jaw dropped when he casually asked if his fiancé could join us. Anger simmered beneath my surface as I resisted the urge to scream, "What the fuck is this, a meet and greet?" It was like being on a fucking field trip, revisiting old lovers and introducing new ones. Defeated once again, I allowed Gage's fiancé to come along, desperate to understand why he had chosen him over me. My heart felt like it was ripping in two as I realized that love truly has a twisted sense of humor. Is this a sign that I shouldn't move on from Gage? What the fuck am I saying he is engaged to a whole man. This whole situation feels insane!

The next morning, Stephen showed up at my door, looking exhausted but with a huge smile on his face. He asked me what happened last night, and I filled him in on the whole story. Stephen was shocked by the craziness of it all and compared it to something out of the Twilight Zone. I mentioned that I had plans to see Gage and his fiancé later that day, but Stephen warned me against it. Despite his advice, I insisted on going, questioning why I would subject myself to this emotional turmoil. I realized that I am an emotional cutter, and I shouldn't be. I don't deserve this hurt but maybe this is what I need to finally close the Gage chapter.

Stephen offered to join me tonight, but I declined and reminded him that he already had plans with Jaden. I wanted one of us to have a good time and savor the beauty of this island. I advised Stephen to get some rest while I headed to the gym to release my pent-up frustration. My desires were conflicting; on one hand, I wanted to please myself, but I didn't because I wanted Gage to help with it. What is happening to me?

I collapsed onto my bed, overwhelmed with emotions. Tears cascaded down my cheeks as I faced the harsh reality that the love of my life was engaged - just not to me. This wasn't the first time he had caused me pain, yet I couldn't seem to break away from him. Why did I continue to love a man who clearly didn't reciprocate those feelings? Am I not deserving of his love, attention, and time? Shaking my head, I forced myself up and made my way to the gym, determined to find some sense of strength and clarity amidst this emotional turmoil.

Night quickly fell and as fate would have it, the restaurant was barely two blocks away from my hotel. With trembling hands, I donned my most alluring attire, feeling both vulnerable and empowered at the same time. Stepping out of my room, I felt like a feast for the senses, ready to face whatever lay ahead. But as I drew closer to the restaurant, a wave of suffocating anxiety washed over me. My heart pounded so hard it felt like it might burst through my chest. Gage had sent me a text message telling me that his fiancé is aware of our history. At least it wouldn't be awkward wondering if his fiancé knew. Also, he wouldn't have to wonder why I'm looking at Gage like he is my man.

As I stepped through the doors of the restaurant, my heart skipped a beat when I spotted Gage across the room. His piercing gaze locked with mine and his trademark dimples flashed as he smiled. The sight of him sent a jolt of electricity through me, but I forced myself to remain composed. I couldn't let my soul be pulled back in by his magnetic pull again. As he approached me, I could feel my feet faltering, but I held myself steady. He enveloped me in a warm hug and for a moment, it was like we were back at his house in Atlanta.

Gage led me over to the table where his fiancé was sitting, his back turned towards us. My eyes took in the elegant setting and the flickering candles casting a soft glow over the room. But then my attention was drawn to Thorne as Gage introduced us, "Chaise, this is my fiancé Thorne." I couldn't help but give him a once-over, my gaze lingering on every detail of his appearance. His name, Thorne, seemed fitting- he exuded sharpness. Our eyes met and there was an instant spark of tension between us. I couldn't quite put my finger on what it was, but something about this man made my senses stand on edge. And suddenly, the name Thorne didn't seem so out of place after all - it felt like he could easily become a thorn in my side or maybe even a thorn in my heart.

Gage is the only one for me, and I can't understand why he doesn't see it. He's my true love, and I've never felt this strongly about anyone before. No matter how hard I try, I can't seem to break free from him. Even coming here to Guam to let go of all my worries and have a good time, he still had a hold on me. It seems like no matter where I go, or how far away from home I am, Gage is always there, holding onto me tightly

Thorne's demeanor was cordial as he extended his hand to me, firmly grasping mine and stating, "It's a pleasure to finally meet you,

Chaise. I've heard so much about you." I couldn't help but respond with a hint of sarcasm, saying, "Well I wish I could say the same." Gage shot me a warning look but chuckled it off. We all took our seats at the table, with Gage sitting across from me and Thorne to my right. I let out a sigh of relief that Thorne didn't choose to sit right next to Gage, as I wasn't quite ready to see them side by side yet. Seeing them grind on each other last night was enough. Honestly, I wasn't prepared for any of this - but here we are. The waiter approached and took our drink orders, and I couldn't resist ordering two strong jack and cokes in preparation for what was sure to be a tense evening.

A wildfire raged within me, but as I looked at Gage, a sense of calm washed over me. Despite everything, I still wanted this man. I had thought that putting myself in this situation would turn me off, but being near him made it feel like his fiancé wasn't even there. Thorne and I made small talk, but my attention was solely focused on Gage. It felt like an electric current ran through my veins whenever he was near. The memories of our past encounters flooded my mind, intensifying my desire for him. I quickly realized that Thorne was probably just as curious to meet me as I was him. I'm sure he wondered who this mysterious ex of Gage was. As the evening went on, the tension between us only grew stronger, like a simmering pot about to boil over.

The music was incredible, and I was feeling quite buzzed. In the span of an hour, I must have had at least five Jack and Cokes. The more I drank, the less I felt. Eventually, I came to the realization that Thorne wasn't a terrible person, but it didn't matter at that point. Despite knowing that Gage was the one at fault, I couldn't help but direct all my anger towards Thorne. Our eyes kept meeting throughout the night, and I'm sure Thorne noticed. I stopped ordering drinks for myself, but Thorne took over and started buying drinks for the whole table. How could I say no? With all the alcohol coursing through my veins, I was hoping for some sort of out-of-body experience.

As the night wore on and I indulged in more drinks, my mind blurred and swam with conflicting emotions. I couldn't deny it, even in my tipsy state - I still wanted Gage. It wasn't supposed to be like this. Before boarding the plane to Guam, I was convinced that I had moved on from him and this chaotic situation. Yet here I am, sitting with the man I love and his fiancé. As they laughed and chatted, a fire of jealousy and anger ignited within me. Was I not good enough to be his fiancé? If only he had waited for me, I would have proposed instead. This intense surge of emotions was foreign to me, leaving me feeling bewildered and lost. Despite it all, I sat there pretending to be okay when I was far from it.

Being a writer isn't my only identity; I also have an inner actor that comes to life in my mind. I had to stay in character, not giving away any hint of my true feelings, because losing control could jeopardize everything, including my career. It took all my willpower not to lash out or cause a scene, but the urge was there - to flip tables and break glasses, releasing my frustration on something tangible. Instead, I turned to alcohol, numbing myself with drinks and even dancing on my chair for a moment. Eventually, I realized I needed to leave and walk back to my room, but Gage and Thorne intervened. They convinced me to let them take me back to my hotel, and I reluctantly agreed.

I stumbled into the backseat of the car, my head spinning from the rush of alcohol and emotions. Thorne's hands gripped the steering wheel as Gage sat silently in the passenger seat. My stomach churned, threatening to expel its contents. Was it the alcohol or the sight of them together that made me feel this way? Either way, I was stuck in a living nightmare. The man I wanted and loved was so close, yet unreachable, while the man who had him was just inches away. I couldn't understand why love would allow this pain to consume me. It felt like emotional torture to see them together. Maybe I should have said no to all of this, but a part of me wanted to see who Gage would choose over me. And despite my best efforts, I couldn't bring myself to hate Thorne - he was still a stranger to me, after all - but at the same time, I couldn't stand him for taking away the love of my life. This situation cut deep into my heart and soul, leaving scars that may never fully heal.

As the car pulled up to my hotel, I could feel the tension building in my chest. Gage was the first to exit, gracefully opening my door and extending his hand to help me out. But it was Thorne who caught me off guard, wrapping me in a warm embrace instead of shaking my hand like a stranger. My mind screamed at me to hate this man, but I didn't. As Thorne moved aside for Gage to come tell me bye, I briefly forgot about Thorne's presence as my body melted into Gage's embrace. It felt like heaven, our bodies pressed together as if trying to merge into one being. But reality came crashing back when I felt Thorne's piercing gaze on us, like a hawk ready to swoop down and attack.

With great effort, I tore myself away from Gage before Thorne could see how much he affected me. Only he had the power to make my soul leave my body and wander aimlessly in the stratosphere. But even after our embrace ended, our eyes locked in a silent exchange filled with longing and desire that was almost disrespectful considering Thorne's presence. The internal battle between my desires and morals raged on within me, making me curse myself for having such conflicting feelings towards Gage.

Watching Gage and Thorne get back into the car, a part of me left with Gage. How I longed to be the one driving off into the night with that beautiful man. If only I was engaged to him, then he would be by my side instead of me stumbling alone to my hotel room. Throughout the night, I couldn't help but wish that I had asked Gage to walk me up, but then again, I wouldn't want him to leave either. And Thorne would be sure to follow along, that would defeat the purpose of asking Gage in the first place. As I rode up in the elevator, thoughts of Stephen and Jaden's whereabouts crossed my mind. At least one of us was getting lucky tonight. Collapsing onto the bed in a drunken haze, I drifted off into a deep sleep.

My eyes snap open, my stomach churning and lurching in protest. The room is a blur of spinning lights and I clutch the sheets, trying to stop the world from tilting. My mouth floods with saliva, a clear warning of what's to come. But I fight it, holding back the overwhelming urge to vomit until I can't bear it any longer. In a panicked frenzy, I stumble towards the bathroom, barely making it to the toilet before my body heaves and convulses, expelling all the alcohol from hours before. Each convulsion feels like torture, but I know it's nothing compared to the torment I endured looking at Gage and Thorne. My regret for drinking is overshadowed by my realization that it was the only way I could've made it through last night.

A knock at my door startled me, and I was surprised to see Stephen standing on the other side. Instead of using the connecting door between our rooms, he must have thought it would be more respectful to knock. It would have been nice if I ended up with Gage like he assumed. But unfortunately, that wasn't the case. My head pounded and I felt nauseous from last night's excessive drinking. As soon as I opened the door,

Stephen walked in, and I rushed to the bathroom to vomit once again. In between bouts of vomiting, I explained what happened last night while Stephen rubbed my back in comfort. He truly was a good friend, always there to support me no matter how bad things got. Before he left to get some hangover remedies, he made sure I was okay. I laid down and fell asleep.

When I awoke, the pounding in my head was almost unbearable. Blinking through bleary eyes, I saw Stephen sitting next to me, a concerned look on his face. Despite feeling like death, I couldn't help but appreciate his presence and the items he had brought to ease my hangover. The room was filled with a faint scent of lavender from the essential oils he had lit. With gentle hands, he helped me sit up and handed me a glass of water and some Advil. As I sipped on the water, Stephen began to recount his wild night with Jaden. His words were animated and full of excitement as he described their adventures. But even through his exhaustion, it was clear that he had enjoyed every minute of it.

Seeing how drained he looked, I insisted that he take a nap before meeting up with Jaden again later that day. He obliged, leaving the adjoining doors between our rooms open just in case I needed him. By the time Stephen woke up, my hangover had subsided, and I was feeling more like myself. As I watched Stephen prepare for his date with Jaden, it made me reflect on my own love life. Who would have guessed that I'd be here, watching him excitedly get ready to see a guy he really liked? He wanted me to come along tonight because he was convinced that I would meet someone new.

Under the stars that night, there we were Stephen, Jaden, and me. The moonlight cast a soft glow on the beach, highlighting the crashing waves and the gentle breeze. Jaden was truly captivating, with a warm smile and sparkling eyes that seemed to shine with genuine kindness. I couldn't help but feel like a proud parent watching their child experience love, seeing how happy Stephen was in his presence. Wanting to give them some time together, I excused myself early and took a walk along the beach. The sand was cool beneath my bare feet and the salty scent of the ocean filled my senses. As I strolled, taking in the beauty around me, I couldn't help but reflect on my own life and this unexpected turn of events. Despite the loving couples scattered along the beach, I felt incredibly alone and far from home. Yet, in that moment, surrounded by nature's wonders, I couldn't help but feel a sense of peace wash over me.

Over the next few days, I was determined to fully immerse myself in the breathtaking beauty of the island. Along with Stephen and Jaden, we embarked on a tour of the island, taking in all its wonders and secrets. However, in the back of my mind, I couldn't help but hope that I wouldn't run into Gage or Thorne. Their presence would only serve as a painful reminder of everything that had transpired. Despite Gage's persistent texts since he and Thorne dropped me off, I chose not to respond. My mind was still reeling from all that had happened, and I needed time to process and make sense of it all.

As our vacation ended, a feeling of homesickness settled over me. Despite the drama with Gage, I couldn't regret taking this getaway. On our last night, I joined Stephen and Jaden for a decadent dinner overlooking the ocean. The colors of the sunset reflected on the water, creating a breathtaking backdrop for our meal. Afterward, I made my way back to my room to pack and give Stephen and Jaden some time alone. The sound of waves crashing against the shore lulled me into a peaceful sleep, and as I drifted off, I couldn't help but look forward to returning home tomorrow.

I couldn't wait to catch up with my friends Kyra and Summer and tell them all about the chaos that had ensued on this trip.

    The next morning, the soft glow of dawn filtered through the curtains as I made my way downstairs to the waiting car. Stephen was already there, ready to head to the airport for our flight back home. Just as we were about to leave, my phone rang with an incoming call from Gage. I hesitated before picking up, unsure if I wanted to hear what he had to say. But curiosity won and I answered. He asked what I was doing, and I told him about our impending trip home. There was a wistful tone in his voice as he expressed his regret that we hadn't been able to spend more time together. I echoed his sentiment but couldn't ignore the weight of our current situation. Fighting back tears, I quickly ended the call, not wanting Gage to hear my emotional state. As Stephen and I arrived at the airport and navigated through security, my mind was filled with thoughts of Gage and our time together. Boarding our first flight out of two, headed back to Atlanta, I couldn't help but feel sadness for what could have been between us.

    We boarded the flight and right before takeoff, I received a text from Gage. He wished me a safe flight and told me he would miss me. I replied with a simple "thank you," and added that I would miss him too. There was no need for any negativity towards someone I truly love. I need to get back home and process everything that has happened. I thought I could avoid Gage, but I ended up running into him anyway, and to make matters worse, he's now engaged. I feel foolish and humiliated. Not only does Gage know that I'm still in love with him, but his fiancé also knows now after the scene I made.

I grit my teeth and clench my fists, steeling myself for the confrontation ahead. LOVE, you have some serious explaining to do. I've always been loyal to you, stood up for you against all odds, but now I'm starting to doubt your existence. As the plane hurtled down the runway, I made a decision. No more playing by your rules, LOVE; it's time for me to take control and break them. You may not play fair, but neither will I.

You may be eager to know what comes next, but that is for another book- one that will shatter expectations and leave you breathless. So, stay tuned and heed this warning: never settle, always fight for what you desire. Because from this day on, I, Chaise Kelley, will stop at nothing to claim my destiny. And to all who have read this far, brace yourselves for the explosive Part 2 that will shake your very core.

TO BE CONTINUED...

• • •
79

Made in the USA
Coppell, TX
12 August 2024

35938651R00044